C000144056

Love, HATE and Indifference

Amelia Watchman

Tamarillas Press

Cover Design: © Amy Mayes Waite
Cover Image: Pixabay

ISBN: 9798641601625

Dedication

To my inspirational mum for her encouragement.
To my wonderful husband for his love and support.
I cannot thank you both enough.

Chapter 1

Message to: Nick
From: Alma
Hey, I know you only just got off the ship but I miss you already. Wish our contracts had matched and I could have got off the ship with you! Can't wait to see you in 2 weeks! Love you. xxxx

Message to: Nick
From: Alma
Hi Nick, we're in Dubrovnik today, feels weird being here without you. How's it being home? Kelly and all the crew say hello. Let me know what time you can pick me up on Saturday for the family meet. Eek! xx

Email to: nickjonessilvine5678z@hotmail.com
From: almajohnson99ax@gmail.com
Hey… so I haven't heard from you, not sure if you're getting my texts so thought I'd email. I bet you're just rushed off your feet at home! My mum's dying to know when we'll get to Twinton. I should be off by midday. I was thinking we could go for a nice lunch in

Southampton before we leave for Twinton? Anyway, message me back. Love you, Alma xxx
Calling Nick ....
Calling Nick....

Nick's answer phone.
'Hi, it's Alma, I'm not sure why you're not answering me, anyway can you let me know what's going on please?'

Message to: Nick
From: Alma
Hi Nick, I'm getting really pissed off now. Are you coming to meet me on Saturday? Kelly thinks you're playing a prank on me, it's not funny. I'll be waiting at the terminal for you, if you're not coming let me know. Alma.

Calling Nick ....
Calling Nick ....
Calling Nick....
'We're sorry; you have reached a number that has been disconnected or is no longer in service. If you feel you have reached this recording in error, please check the number and try your call again.'

Chapter 2

One year later

'Time to get back on that horse. Come on, I can write you a killer profile that will have everyone messaging!' Sara gives me a wicked grin and begins to stab at her laptop while Denise looks on in silence.

I turn to face Sara who stops and inspects her wine glass. 'I'm not sure, isn't internet dating for hooking up with ugly men pretending to be someone else, catfishing is it? I'm not really into that. Why can't I meet someone organically?'

Sara rolls her eyes and wipes her long hair from her face. 'Perhaps once upon a time but not now, no one meets in a bar anymore. It's time to get with it, Alma. It's been long enough and you *haven't* met anyone organically. I'm going to be brutally honest; it's just depressing now.'

I go over to the fridge and grab a fresh bottle of wine and offer it to my two friends. Denise shakes her head. 'You know, I understand you've not been ready but I think Sara may be right, although not entirely about the depressing part.' Denise, ever the mediator, never wants to offend, so if even she thinks it's time, it must mean it is. 'And besides, may I remind you that's how I met my partner.'

Whoops. 'I know Denise, but you and Jay met through mutual friends on Facebook, it wasn't exactly internet dating but more of a modern day set up.' I turn back to Sara. 'Okay, fine, do the profile, but don't make me sound stupid, I want it to reflect who I really am. I don't want them to be disappointed or think I'm an airhead.' I sigh and slump down on one of the breakfast stools, pouring myself a large glass of wine. If I have to do this, I'm going to need some Dutch courage.

Sara looks like the cat that got the cream. 'No problem! But we do need a little embellishment, there's no harm in that. Just you with a bit of sizzle, oh and an amazing profile pic.' With that Sara holds her phone up to my face and snaps, she looks down at her phone and pulls a face that suggests it does not look good. 'Okay, we need to work on that too. Perhaps some make-up.'

Two hours later and after a copious amount of wine, I have my first dating profile set up on *meant2b* dating. I'm feeling a bit pleased with myself; I don't sound half bad.

Alma, 27 from Twinton
About me
A photographer of life and a traveller of places, fun loving, kind and adventurous. Friends and family are important to me and keep a smile on my face.

Things I like
Love the outdoors and spending time with my friends. A keen art lover and wine drinker.

Looking for
An ambitious, caring man who has an adventurous side and an interest in travel. I'm not looking for casual hook ups so if that's you, jog on.

'Are you sure the profile is really me though, Sara?' I put my head in my hands feeling momentarily unsure. 'I mean, I'm not really a photographer or a traveller anymore. I've been at home for nearly a year working at Holborns.' Holborns is our local bank, at first, I took the job for the money and after a year I can *definitely* say I go there for the money. Administration is absolutely not my calling. I did love my job as a photographer and had things turned out differently that's where I would be now. I can feel my cheeks colour with the memory of the humiliation and I brush the thoughts from my mind like a cobweb. I'm moving on, I don't want to think about all of that or *him*. Nick.

'Yes, darling but that job is not who you are! You have a hundred stories, and I didn't say you were a photographer, I said you photograph life, that's ambiguous and intriguing enough. Trust me.'

I look to Denise for support, we've spent the last fifteen minutes creating the text for my profile. The rest of the time has been spent creating the perfect profile picture which has consisted of me trying on everything in my cupboard twice over and then wearing the outfit Sara had on which is far too long on me as, at 5ft 10 inches she towers over my meagre 5ft 4. But it's okay as you can only see my face anyway. We select a few and use an old photograph of me from my days working on a cruise ship as my main picture.

'I just don't want them to be disappointed when they see that the real thing is not quite as nice or interesting as my profile. Look how pale I am now for a start.' I stroke my arm and instantly miss my tan, with olive skin and dark hair as soon as the summer comes, I get a little colour but in these photos my skin is positively glowing from months in the Caribbean sun, I look practically Mediterranean.

'Ah, Alma, they won't be. Okay, so you're not a photographer anymore, but you are qualified and maybe you're not travelling at the moment but you have travelled a great deal. It's a conversation starter and who cares about a tan, it's only April for goodness sake, no one expects you to have a year-round tan, even if it has been unseasonably warm over the last few days.'

'That's true,' Sara chips in, 'And there's no way they'd be disappointed, anyone would be lucky to have you and everyone embellishes, no one puts "sits around watching teen mom in my old granny underwear" in their profile, do they?'

'Ummm, for the record I don't do that,' I say, frowning at Sara.

'Never said you did, darling,' Sara says innocently, staring pointedly at my bra strap, or *the over the shoulder boulder holder* as she referred to it when I changed into her dress. I tuck my strap into my top, perhaps it's time to get some new underwear too.

'Okay, let's do this but I'm holding you both personally responsible if it all goes wrong!' I glare at them so they know I'm serious and they both plaster a smile on their face; it's nice to have two people who are so confident in me, on my side.

Just then I hear the jingle of keys and the door slam. Surely Mum and Dad aren't home already.

'Mum, are you here, I need to… oh, hello.' My older

sister Jenna walks into the room and appraises us. We're sat at the island in the middle of the kitchen with our glasses of wine and Sara's laptop. 'What are you up to?' My sister flicks her long blonde hair and clip clops on the slate flooring around to the laptop, she sticks her hand in as I try to shut it and spots my profile. She sneers. 'Oh God, you haven't resorted to internet dating, have you? I didn't know you were *that* desperate.'

I feel my face flush, I knew this was a bad idea. God, I feel stupid. Jenna has arrived and single handily burst my bubble, my cheeks begin to glow hot and it's not just from the wine.

'Actually, Jenna, I've met many a suitable man online, I'll have you know and I am *anything* but desperate.' Sara comes to my rescue and I look at her with warmth, thank goodness for good friends. If there's one thing you could not accuse Sara of being it is desperate. Self-assured, tall, beautiful and painfully honest she could charm the skin off a snake and remembering some of her exes perhaps that's exactly what she has done.

Jenna gawps after Sara's rebuke, but quickly recovers. 'You're right, it's a different age now to when I was dating. Come on then, let me have a look. Who knows you better than big sis?' She spins the laptop round and silently reads as a myriad of expressions cross her face. Finally, she says, 'Are you sure you don't want it to be a bit more current, I mean you're not even doing photography anymore or travelling, although I suppose administration at Holborns doesn't sound very exciting either'. She laughs and grabs a wine glass, then fills it from the bottle of white on the worktop. The cheek of her.

'Jenna, don't you have somewhere else to be, who's looking after the kids? And Dave?' I say, annoyed at her muscling in on our evening. 'Mum and Dad have gone to the cinema. Did you want to leave a message with me?' I hope she'll take the hint and leave. Ten years my senior, we were thick as thieves when we were younger and I idolised her. She was my hero but as we've grown up, we've grown apart which makes me sad when most of my friends seem to get closer to their siblings as they age. Jenna's perfect life is so VERY hard to compete with.

'Nope, nowhere to be, the kids are teenagers so they can look after themselves and Dave is doing a spot of work in the home office. They're thinking of making him partner you know. So he's working lots of late nights at the moment.' She smiles and I can see she has regained her air of superiority.

'Well, we've just uploaded the profile so we're waiting to see who responds now and then we'll have a look at the men. I think it sums up Alma perfectly, it's about who she is not what she does.' Denise smiles sweetly and I'm reassured that this could be the bit of fun I was looking for. I haven't dated in the past year so it would be nice to get back out there and meet someone, maybe.

'Okay, sounds fun, you don't mind me sticking around do you, Alma? Be lovely to hang out with you and the girls. Tell me, how does it work?' Jenna smiles serenely and looks innocuously at me, what can I do? Of course, I'm going to let her stay.

'Well, you go through multiple profiles and if you like the look or sound of them you press the tick and if you don't like them you press the cross. If they press the tick too then you have a *meant2b* match and the app lets you know so you can talk,' I explain.

'We're going to take a vote per man as Ms Fussy over there…' Sara nods her head towards me, 'Seems to want to say no to every man on here which is not the point of this.' She eyes me suspiciously as she knows I'm trying to prolong the planning of going on a date as opposed to the actual going.

'Yes, so it's majority rules,' Denise explains further. 'Although now there are four of us, what will we do in a tie breaker situation?' Denise looks questioningly to Sara, the natural leader of the pack, to make the call.

'Well obviously I should have the deciding vote,' I interject. 'After all, I am the one going on the date!'

'No, darling, I get the deciding vote, because you are predisposed to say no and we're getting you out of your comfort zone. Whoever you date doesn't need to be your future husband. After all, you have to kiss a few frogs to find a prince.'

'Sounds good to me,' Jenna agrees. 'Now let's have a look at the men. Wow, this is so much fun. I've never looked at one of these sites before, it's so *weird* to think this is how people meet.' She emphasises the weird and casts her eyes over at me.

I'm not going to rise to the implied dig. It's fine, I'm going to have a laugh with my girls. I take a big sip of my drink, my head is slightly swimming from all of the wine, so maybe it is best that Sara has final choice. Although if any of her ex-boyfriends are anything to go by, I'll be dating a hippy, punk or biker by the end of this. Sara definitely likes a bit of a bad-boy-outsider vibe but that really is not my thing. Hopefully we can find one suitable guy, I can put off going on the date for long enough for him to lose interest and the girls will forget about it. I'm fine on my own after all, I'm a strong, independent woman… or something like that.

'Now, it's a game of numbers,' Sara explains. 'We need to look through lots of profiles before we'll find the one.'

We all gather around the laptop, set on our mission to find a man, I think I'd enjoy it rather more if we were looking for someone else but as it's me, I meet it with a touch of hesitation.

We spend the next hour looking at profile after profile, from the mundane self-depreciating good-guy, the gym going hot bod with no personality who'll probably bore me with how much time he has spent at the gym and what he has eaten that day – doesn't everyone start the day with six eggs – to the computer geeks, funny guys, seemingly normal and bad boys. There's someone for everyone. We agree to hit tick on five guys, the final one was a tiebreaker, Denise and I said no but Sara and Jenna said yes and as Sara has the deciding vote it didn't end in my favour.

Much to my surprise all of the guys tick me too, except the final one so I guess I won that in the end. In spite of myself I've really had a good time looking at all of the profiles. Jenna has warmed up, removed the stick from up her arse and joined in with lots of laughs too and it's been kind of nice to spend some time with her for a change.

'Shall we wait and see who messages you, or should we message them straight off,' Jenna asks.

'Let's send something to them, how about a funny line?' Sara suggests.

'What kind of line? Like a chat up line?' I gawp at Denise, what have I let myself in for.

'Yeah, what about if you were an apple, you'd be a golden delicious?' says Sara, this is probably a line that's been used on her.

'No. That's an absolute no. Thank you for the suggestion but I think we'll wait and see if they message me first. And for the record, *I'm* deciding this as I'm the one who'll be going on the date.'

Suddenly my profile pings with two messages. The first one is from Henderson, a cute, cheeky guy who likes mountain biking, adventure and the outdoors. I nervously click on the message and wait to see what he has said, but instead of a 'Hello' or 'Hi' there's an image. A very inappropriate image.

'Well I certainly wouldn't call those apples delicious!' Sara bursts into laughter and then we're all at it, that was certainly not what I was expecting from internet dating. Once I pull myself together, I ask, 'Is it normal to send that?'

'Sometimes,' Sara replies. 'But don't get put off the rest of the men from one horny dog. Let's look at the other message, I'm sure it couldn't be any worse.'

I click on the second message, it's from Lewis, a teacher with lovely hazel eyes and a great smile, he has done some travelling, is keen to do more and has a passion for art. Thankfully there is no image of his golden delicious this time, just a simple message.

Hello, nice to meet you, I'm Lewis. Would be great to chat or go for a drink? I think we have some shared interests.

'This is great!' Sara exclaims. 'He's already asked you on a date so we just need to arrange the when and where now.'

'Woah, I wasn't expecting that. I thought we'd just chat for a bit first and then much later, maybe weeks, go on the date.' My plan of letting it peter out and the girls forgetting about it isn't going well, I may actually have to *go* on a date.

'Move aside, we're going to respond,' Sara commands.

Denise shoves the computer over to Sara and at the same time gives me an apologetic smile. 'We'll set up the date then all you have to do is go on it, we can help do your hair and make-up before.'

Sara types furiously and pauses. 'How is Sunday for you?'

'Sunday is tomorrow, isn't this moving a bit too fast? I say in a panic. 'What if he's a serial killer? Shouldn't we do our due diligence?'

'It's fine, I've arranged for you to meet in a nice busy bar, there will be plenty of people there, nothing to worry about.' Her smile broadens with an idea. 'We could always come and sit in the corner.'

Jenna's head flicks up evidently finding the idea appealing. Yes, I'm sure they'd all love that, gawping at me like an exhibit, but I can't think of anything worse.

'No way! I'll do the date but you three are not coming to watch and laugh at me in the corner, I'll be nervous enough as it is.'

Denise looks at me reassuringly. 'We won't come, don't worry.'

Chapter 3

It's Sunday afternoon and I'm meeting Lewis at 7.30 this evening at a slightly too trendy for me bar in the old part of town. Sara picked the location but I wish I'd picked it myself now as I feel totally out of my comfort zone, but honestly, I couldn't think of anywhere to go. I obviously don't get out enough.

I hear a knock at the door and Denise is the first to arrive with a reassuring smile and a great array of make-up, she may not be as bold as Sara but she is always subtly flawless. Her style feels a lot more me so I'm pleased she's doing my make-up. Sara would probably put so much on he'd wonder if I was impersonating a clown. The girls all agreed I needed help to get ready but I think they secretly wanted to make sure I didn't cancel the date. Denise pushes her glasses up onto her nose and sweeps her fringe away.

'Right, let's get started, shall we?' she asks. I lead her through to my room and as I sit down in front of my antique dressing table, I brush my hand over the painted wood. I love this find; it feels so totally me. I spent a long few days fixing it up with Mum and it makes me smile every time I look at it.

Mum definitely knows something is going on and keeps hovering in the hallway outside my room. This is when I really hate living at home. Mum is like a homing pigeon, trying to pick up any little scraps of information. It's almost impossible to keep a secret from her. I remember when I had my first boyfriend; I was only twelve, all shy and embarrassed about it but she worked me out almost instantly. She knew there was something different and it was about a boy. I feel exactly like that now. Dad on the other hand will be wandering around in his own world. He won't care what's going on as long as I'm happy. He doesn't ask the awkward questions and that's something I've always liked about him.

Jenna arrives shortly after Denise and I can hear Mum chattering away trying to find out what's going on, fortunately Jenna brushes her off and heads upstairs. Thank goodness for that, Jenna actually has my back for a change. I don't want Mum asking me how the date was, what if he turns out to be a forty-five-year-old grandad? Or worse.

Mum met Dad at school, childhood sweethearts, the only man Mum has ever loved. Internet dating would feel completely foreign to her and I think she'd worry I'd be kidnapped or murdered. Mum's a worrier which she feeds with her incessant reading of the scare stories in the papers, she's always warning us to travel in groups and look out for each other. It's sweet really.

Denise, Jenna and I stay shut up in my room. Jenna has brought a bottle of wine and we pop it open. I resign myself to only having one this time. I don't want to be drunk when I meet my date, that would be a disaster and besides I may need my wits about me if

Mum is to be believed. Denise expertly does my make-up while Jenna looks through my wardrobe.

'You don't really have much for a date, there are a lot of jeans in here,' Jenna notes, roughly cling clanging the hangers across the rail.

'Well I want to be comfortable; a nice top and jeans would do surely?' I used to wear a lot of dresses, in fact that was one of the things that Nick had really liked about me. There he is again. Nick. Why am I even thinking about him? Who cares what that prick likes?

'Hmmm.' Jenna exchanges a look with Denise. 'When is Sara getting here?'

'I'm not sure, you know Sara. Why, what's the matter?' I look from Denise to Jenna for reassurance. 'Surely it's not *that* bad?'

'Nothing, nothing, we'll find something don't worry. What are you doing with your hair?' I wish she hadn't said that, I'm really starting to doubt myself.

'It's done, doesn't it look done?' I swish my head looking between Denise and Jenna while Denise tries to keep my head steady. I can feel the panic rise in my chest. So far, the only thing that's right seems to be my face and that's because Denise is doing it. I thought he was going on a date with *me* but I can't even do my own make-up and hair and my clothes are all wrong, apparently.

'Oh um, well at least your face will look nice.' Jenna grins, she couldn't resist one little dig. Why did I let her come over?

'It's fine Alma, your hair looks good, but you could make a bit more effort, maybe.' Denise is expertly applying my eye shadow and it's taking a painstakingly long time, she is definitely thorough, I'll give her that. Normally make-up takes me fifteen minutes max and that includes washing my face.

'Oh God, you guys are supposed to be helping me and you're making me feel more nervous. According to you my hair and clothes are awful. This is how I normally wear my hair; I just want to look like me,' I whinge, slumping my shoulders like a moody teen.

My hair is thick and golden brown with a mind of its own. I've washed it and put it up into a bun to keep its unruliness at bay. It's my preferred style and I thought over time I had perfected it so that it looks casual but good and maybe even, stylish. Clearly not. I'm having some hard lessons tonight. I thought getting ready for a date with your girls was all giggling and trying on clothes but this is becoming rather an eye-opening experience. Now I know what everyone really thinks.

'I only really wear it down for special occasions, you know Christmas and that,' I explain, hoping they'll back down and assure me it's actually fine.

'Well you wear it down at some other times too. It's down in your profile picture. Anyway, this is your first date in over a year, how is this not a special occasion? Why don't you let me do it for you?' Jenna asks.

'She's right, Alma, we just want you to feel like the best you. It's nice to look good and feel great about yourself,' Denise adds. I suppose she's right. I could make a bit more of an effort, I just don't want to end up looking like a dog's dinner.

'Fine, but don't do anything too crazy with it,' I plead, giving Jenna a hard stare.

Jenna comes over and starts picking at my hair, although we are sisters, we look quite different and in particular our hair. Jenna's hair is blonde and much thinner than mine. I'm not really sure she'd know what to do with mine but, not wanting to offend her, I let her have a go. I hadn't quite prepared myself for a full makeover tonight, I just hope Lewis is worth it. He did look really cute in his profile picture, very manly with a strong jawline and a smattering of stubble. I doubt it's taking him this amount of time to get ready though. I bet he's not had an entourage of people picking apart *his* appearance.

After further scrutiny of my clothes we all agree on a pretty green top with lace around the bottom and blue skinny jeans. I put my foot down on footwear, I do not want to wear heels, they'll just be a hindrance *if* I do need to make a quick getaway. Finally, we settle on some plain black ballet pumps.

An hour later I'm dressed and feeling pretty decent. Jenna has pulled it out of the bag and my hair is looking really quite good, she's given it a soft wave with a clip pulling it off my face to one side. I didn't know she was so talented with hair and make a mental note to enlist her for any future events. Perhaps the girls were right, maybe this date will be okay. At least I look the part now. I feel pretty good too.

Sara finally arrives, fashionably late, banging on the front door and ready to make an entrance, she's wearing a red wrap dress with towering leopard print heels. She must be off on her own date afterwards, which wouldn't surprise me as she's a serial dater. On arrival she assesses me when Denise and I answer the door, looking me up and down with a frown on her face and her lips pursed.

'No, darling, no. This is not what you're wearing. Make-up looks good, although you could do with a bit more eye shadow and lippy.' She gives Denise a cheeky smile. 'Hair is nice, good to see you wearing it down for a change. You look *almost* date ready. It's just the outfit.

Fortunately, I have a selection of garments….' She winks as she lifts up her hands to reveal two bursting carrier bags in each hand. 'I remembered the sad state of your wardrobe from the last time,' she says by way of an explanation.

Oh God, I need to leave in thirty minutes. If getting ready is this stressful then Lewis had better be worth it.

As we make our way upstairs Mum's at it again peering round the door. 'Oh hello, Sara, it's getting packed in that room now. What's going on in there?' I eye Sara trying to signal to her to keep her mouth closed but she's oblivious.

'Alma's got a date, first one in a year,' she sings merrily. The jig is up, of course Sara would be the one to let the cat out of the bag. She has no shame and wouldn't understand why I'd be embarrassed to tell Mum. Sara and her own mum are thick as thieves, she tells her everything. Too many things sometimes.

Mum played her hand well; she was probably waiting for Sara all along. She's known Sara since she was eleven years old and Sara had the same amazing confidence then that she has now. On our first day at secondary school she approached me, declared that having just moved to the area she knew no one, and that we were to be friends and was I free for a sleepover at the weekend. I thought she was glorious; I'd never seen someone so self-assured. I was shy and awkward mumbling yes please.

I glare at Mum and mumble. 'Yes, I've got a date. I've got to go in a minute so we can't stop.' I shove Sara into the room and she stumbles in all arms and legs with the four bags of clothes flying everywhere.

'Right, we need all hands on deck. Alma can't go out like that.' Sara nods her head towards me and I feel like a five-year-old who has decided to wear a fancy-dress costume to go to the shops.

'Oh, and the shoes, you need heels. What have you got?' I roll my eyes, here we go again.

Everyone rummages and rustles through the bags. A huge clothes mountain appears on my floor. Sorting through them all creates a kaleidoscope of colours and fabrics, each outfit more daring than the next. Sara pulls out a leopard print mini dress. 'What about this, I love this. It would look great on you.'

Jenna stifles a snigger as I politely decline. It's Denise who finally finds it. A knee length, green polka dot, shirt dress, cinched in at the waist with a matching belt. I try it on and under duress team it up with some heeled boots that were at the bottom of my wardrobe. One of Sara's black leather jackets finishes off the look and actually, I reluctantly admit, this is better than my original outfit.

'You look great, Alma.' Denise smiles her approval and Sara and Jenna enthusiastically nod in agreement. Finally! I'm ready.

'Let's just undo those top two buttons, you don't need it done up to your chin, you're not a nun.' Sara comes over and flicks the buttons undone. 'Right then, I'm off,' she says.

'Don't you want your clothes?' I grimace at the mass of clothing on my bedroom floor. It looks like my teenage niece's bedroom with barely an inch of carpet visible. What an absolute mess. There's also make-up and hair products everywhere. It's going to take me ages to clean up. I shake my head as I look at the destruction these three have left.

'No, it's fine. I'll collect them later. After all, I need to hear all about this date. I better be off, places to be, things to do.' And with that Sara breezes out as quickly as she came in.

Jenna wishes me luck and heads downstairs. I'm sure now Mum knows what I'm up to she'll be quizzing Jenna all evening about my date.

Denise gives me a lift but with all the faffing about with the clothes I'm already running a bit late. I hope he doesn't mind. Surely, it's a woman's prerogative to be late on the first date.

I arrive at the Moon bar and glance around looking for Lewis. I'm almost ten minutes late and I'm feeling nervous. Perhaps because I'm so late he has already left; would that really be so bad? I look down and fumble to do up the top two buttons of my dress, much better.

The bar is packed. If there was any doubt before, now I'm sure that Sara picked it. It's very much her taste, stylish and modern. All the tables are taken and the atmosphere is loud and buzzing. There are a few people sitting at the bar, all with their backs to me. A woman dressed from head to toe in black with a large fedora hat catches my attention in particular. She's either a millionaire's widow or a lady of the night, either way she looks rather odd.

At that moment Lewis approaches me and I lose my train of thought. He looks just like his profile picture and has very warm eyes and a friendly smile. He's wearing a pale blue shirt, sleeves rolled up to show off his toned arms perfectly. I'm instantly reassured and I relax as he leans in to give me a kiss on the cheek and introduce himself.

We go to the bar and get a couple of drinks and

head out into the beer garden to enjoy the warm spring night. It doesn't feel so trendy out here and I feel much more in my comfort zone. We finally find a table facing into the bar. I begin to feel nervous again, it's time for small talk. There's an awkward pause where we both think about what to say next.

'I'm so sorry I was late,' I say trying to make it obvious I'm not some diva who's always late. I bet Sara would never apologise for being late on a date.

'Don't worry at all,' he reassures me. 'I'm just relieved you're here; another five minutes and I was about to approach the lady in black with the hat at the bar.' He subtly points to where she's sat. 'She was the only woman I could see alone. Although, I was a bit scared of her to be honest. Do you think she's come from a funeral or is maybe a mobster's wife?' He smiles and it lightens his face, he really is rather good looking.

I laugh and it instantly breaks the ice. I begin to feel myself relax again. I look over to the bar, I can see black fedora hat still nursing a drink. I have a better view of her now and I can see that she's wearing a tight midi dress and jacket, perhaps the most intriguing thing about her is she's wearing sunglasses, inside. Admittedly, it's a warm and bright evening but she's inside the bar so those sunglasses are completely pointless. Mobster's wife may not be wrong, I smirk to myself. She really does look rather ridiculous, what is she trying to hide from?

I look down to her shoes and I see them. Leopard print heels. That's when I realise that I recognise that lady in black. That lady in black was at my house a mere half hour ago. No wonder she had to leave so suddenly, she needed to change into that bizarre outfit and get here before me. And to think she took the mick out of what *I* was wearing. The funny thing is, if she'd worn something normal, I may not have even noticed her.

Sara.

Chapter 4

Sara has completely thrown me. I can't believe she's here. I'm absolutely seething. I've half a mind to walk over to her right now but I don't really want to associate with her. I'm trying to make a good impression here and she looks absolutely crazy. What was she thinking? What would Lewis think? And what the hell is she wearing? She could at least have changed her shoes.

I try to concentrate on what Lewis is talking about, something about his family, but my eyes keep drifting over to the bar. I find I'm constantly sipping my wine to distract myself. I've virtually downed it and we've only been here ten minutes. Thanks Sara, now I look like an alcoholic. This is not a good start to the date. At this rate I'll be drunk. I look over at Lewis's drink, it's almost full. Well, it's the only thing I can think of...I'll go and get us, well, me, some more drinks.

'Wow, I guess I'm really thirsty,' I say, inspecting my glass. 'I'll go get us some more drinks, and maybe a water for me too.' I giggle, hoping I don't sound completely insane. 'What would you like?'

Lewis looks amused and meaningfully plays with his pint. 'I'm okay ta, but I don't mind getting you another one if you like?' What a gentleman offering to buy another drink when he hasn't even finished his first.

'No, no, don't be silly.' I leap out of my seat before Lewis can persuade me otherwise and practically run to the bar.

♥♥♥

Even though it would make more sense to order the drink from this side of the bar, I purposefully walk all the way round to where Sara is sitting, and slam my purse down on the bar. I look cautiously over at where Lewis is seated, desperately trying to determine if he is looking this way but another person is blocking my view. Great. I'm optimistic he can't see us, well, I have my fingers crossed anyway.

Sara turns to look at me, removing the sunglasses from her face and giving me a sheepish grin and a wink. She knows she's been busted and that I'm *not* happy.

'Don't look at me,' I hiss. I fix my stare straight ahead and clench my jaw. 'What the fuck are you doing here? You promised you wouldn't come.' The more I think about it the more livid I feel. I would never do this to her and they all promised they wouldn't come. The cheek of her.

As instructed, she keeps her head facing towards the bar. 'We promised the *three* of us wouldn't come, darling. I said nothing about me coming alone.' She giggles before continuing. 'He's really cute although you look a bit tense. Try relaxing, calm down a bit. Another drink is a good idea.' Her voice is light and airy trying to soothe me but really, she's fanning the flames.

'*You* are the one stopping me from relaxing, you need to leave. Now. Why do you look so ridiculous anyway? Were the hat and sunglasses really necessary?' I can't help my head from turning Sara's way to take in her bizarre outfit again.

'I'm incognito, darling. I didn't think you'd notice me,' she croons. 'Look, I'm sorry.' Her tone changing as she realises how cross I am. 'I'll go. I don't want to put you off. Just do me one little favour and…' She leans over and flicks open the top two buttons of my dress.

I glare at her hoping that it's enough to convey how I feel about her touching me right now. As I begin to do the buttons back up, she clambers down from her seat and goes, leaving a full martini on the bar. Would it be wrong to take that with me back to our table? Deciding against it I finally catch the barman's attention and order my wine and water.

As I walk back over to our table the sun is beginning to go down. It's looking really rather pretty out here. There are fairy lights, old wooden benches with trendy cushions, and sofas in the beer garden. As I take my seat, Lewis's puzzled expression confirms my worst fears. He definitely saw me talk to Sara. I thank my lucky stars I didn't bring her martini back. How would it look to take some random person's drink?

'Everything okay? Did I see the mobster's wife undo your dress?' Well there's certainly nothing wrong with his observational skills. He has a look of concern in his eyes. I'm sure from a bystander's point of view she has almost just assaulted me. Thanks again, Sara.

'Oh, um yeah, she was just being friendly. She thought it would look better. What was I supposed to do? I don't want her to set her mobster husband on me.' I laugh trying to make light of the situation and pray that he'll drop it so we can get on with our evening.

He gives me a full belly laugh which makes me like him even more and then we settle into a rather lovely evening. Now Sara has gone I'm feeling a lot more comfortable, although I'm sure the wine has helped. The atmosphere is good and the company is even better and I'm really starting to enjoy myself.

Over the course of a few hours, we drink, laugh and get to know each other. He tells me about teaching. He's an art teacher so we definitely have a lot in common. It's lovely to hear about the work that his students are doing at the moment and the exhibitions he has been to and the future ones he is excited about. I can tell he doesn't just teach art, it's also a real passion for him and I love how talking about it makes his face light up and the way he uses big hand gestures to convey how everything makes him feel.

I tell him how I worked as a photographer on a cruise ship and admit that I now work in Holborns, which isn't where I want to be. He's very encouraging and understanding, and tells me how he wanted to be a videographer but it was so difficult because of how competitive it was and I begin to feel a real connection with him. It's nice to date someone who understands what it's like.

I enjoy telling him about the beautiful countries I've visited and he asks lots of questions about where I would visit again, where I would never return to and what life was like living on a cruise ship. He looks at me with awe as I tell him all about my experiences and how it was time to leave, but I omit the real reason I left.

Nick.

We talk more about our families and he tells me all about his sister and niece. His niece's Dad isn't in the picture and for a short while his sister lived with him after her relationship broke down. It's meant he has a lovely bond with his niece, more like a surrogate Dad rather than an uncle. I can see he's a really warm and kind person because I'm sure not everyone would do that for their sister. I tell him about my parents and sister and he laughs at my mum being so nosy before I left the house. I can't quite believe how well the evening is going and I'm really excited at the prospect of getting to know more about him. Reluctantly I have to admit the girls were right. I definitely needed to get myself back out on the dating scene. I'm glad I've made an effort. The girls were right, it's good to look nice.

Nick. Nick who?

The sky has turned into a deep dark blue, with the clouds rolling in. My light jacket is no longer doing its job. I shiver and wrap my arms around myself rubbing furiously to warm up, but I'm not ready to leave yet.

'Are you cold? Do you want to head inside? I could get us some more drinks?' He smiles and I'm pleased our evening isn't coming to an end yet. My head is a little bit woozy from all the wine.

'Sounds great, I'll just have a soft drink. Let's head in. I just need to pop to the loo,' I say.

'Great, I'll go to the bar and find us a seat inside. Hopefully in one of the booths.' As we walk in, side by side, he casually takes my hand in his, wrapping his large fingers around mine. His hand feels warm and manly against my cold fingers and the gesture seems easy and natural. I think the date is going well. It seems crazy that we've only just met. It feels like we've known each other for longer.

Once inside we both pause at the bottom of the stairs and turn towards each other, the toilets are at the top of the stairs. Unexpectedly he leans in and brushes his lips gently across mine. It's the perfect first kiss. I have butterflies in my stomach. I definitely think we could have a second date. I stumble going up the stairs and know that I must look like a right galumph but I can't wipe the smile off my face. I feel giddy with excitement at the prospect of another kiss. A goodnight kiss.

Once in the loos I WhatsApp the girls; Denise had helpfully set up a group called "Alma goes on a date", I'm going to get her to change that once this is over.

WhatsApp: Alma goes on a date

Alma: Date going well although there was this crazy woman at the
start.

Sara: Sorry again, so glad it's going well! He was super cute.

Denise: Huh? Am I missing something? Sara did you go?

Alma: YES, she did! I've not forgiven you yet and you owe me!!

Jenna: Glad it's going well. Mum is asking me about it. Can I tell her anything? Might stop her from asking you when you get back?

Alma: No. I'll talk to her myself, let her stew. She's so nosy!

Denise: So, how is it going?

Alma: Put it this way, he just kissed me. So, I think

we can say it's

   going well.

   Sara: Wooo! That's amazing!

   Denise: So glad it's going well.

   Jenna: Can't wait to hear more, sounds like a very good first date

   Sara: I knew it was time to get back out there!!! ☺

I come out of my toilet cubicle and wash my hands at the long fancy row of sinks. Someone has spent a lot of time decorating these toilets and there are even fancy soaps and hand cream. There's a small sofa over to the side, I guess this is ideal if you come here on a double date and want to chat about your date with your girlfriend. I look over at the girl standing at the basin next to me. She looks awkwardly down at her clothes and I notice she is wearing the exact same dress as me. Oh my God. In fact, her hair and even her boots are similar to mine, and she's wearing a jacket that's the same colour as mine. It's like a version of who wore it best. I'm not sure I would win this one.

'Nice dress,' she says, giggling.

'Yes, you too.' I giggle back, smoothing my dress down and messing with my hair.

I can see we're both ready to go downstairs but we'd look so weird if we went down together, a deranged set of twins. The staircase goes right into the middle of the bar so we'd make quite an entrance.

'You go first, I'll wait a few minutes then go,' I say and see the relief wash over her face.

'Oh, thank you, I was just thinking how weird we'd look,' she says, heading for the door.

I wait a good five minutes then head out. The place seems to have filled up since I went to the toilet and I can't see Lewis over the hordes of people at the bar. I survey the room some more and decide he must have been served and found a table. I begin to walk around, there are lots of nooks and crannies so it takes me quite a while. Checking under the stairs and all along the windows, through to the back, scanning each and every table as I go. I double check the booths. I just can't seem to see Lewis anywhere.

I head back outside, perhaps he couldn't find a seat and came back out. I look at the empty seat where we sat a mere ten minutes ago and a sinking feeling begins to develop. I head back in and begin to do the rounds again. This time I really search along the bar. Then under the stairs, along the windows, through to the back and into all the nooks and crannies. As I go, I can see some of the people I have already passed watching me curiously. I must look a right sight wandering around aimlessly.

I go back outside again, perhaps he's popped to the toilets? I was in there for quite a while after all, probably more than ten minutes. I think about walking back up the stairs but I already feel like I'm drawing too much attention to myself and that everyone is looking at me. I head back in for the final time but I can already feel tears building in my eyes, my heart is beginning to pound in my ears and I know.

Lewis isn't in the toilets. Lewis isn't at the bar. Lewis isn't at the tables or in the back or in any of the nooks and crannies. Lewis isn't outside. Lewis isn't here at all. Lewis has left. Lewis left when I went to the toilets.

I thought the date was going well, but the perfect kiss was actually a goodbye kiss.

Chapter 5

I weave my way back through the tables to the door. As I walk past a table for the third time a man stops me.

'You alright love, have you lost someone?' He looks at me kindly and I put my head down because the tears are so close to brimming over. I'm only just holding myself together and the kindness of strangers makes it worse.

'I'm fine,' I mumble and walk away as quickly as I can. As I pass through the door the big, fat, hot tears finally come. They slide down my face like a slug and I can't bear to be in the bar any longer. I can't bear people being able to see me, they must have worked it out by now too. Who walks around the bar that many times? The humiliation comes in a huge wave over my body.

I walk out into the car park, it's full of cars but there's a line of trees on the far edge. I walk into the trees and sit down on the grass; I feel the dew seeping through my dress and tights. The weather has really turned whilst I've been inside, it exactly mirrors my mood and small droplets of rain begin to fall. I consider getting a taxi so I don't have to speak to anyone but instantly dismiss it. I'll still have to talk to the taxi driver even if only to tell him where I'm going, and knowing my luck I'll get the chattiest of the bunch.

I'm just so confused by it all. Why kiss me if he was going to just leave me? Oh my God, am I a bad kisser? Is that why he left? Perhaps he kissed me and realised he didn't feel anything and so made his escape when the opportunity arose. I feel stupid for having butterflies. I feel stupid for thinking about a second date, for getting ahead of myself. Most of all I feel stupid for going on this date at all. I was right, I should have stuck with my original plan and held off until the girls had forgotten about it. We jumped the gun and now look what's happened.

I message Denise, my designated driver for the evening.

Alma: Could you come and get me please?
Denise: Oh that was quick, everything ok? I'll be about ten minutes.
Alma: He left.
Denise: What?
Denise: What do you mean he left? Are you okay? I'm leaving right now.

I put my phone down; I don't have the energy to explain any further. But I do have the energy for something else; I go onto *meant2b* and delete my profile, so much for internet dating. I also block and delete his phone number. Sara would only want to try and call him once she finds out and I can't face it. What would he say? Perhaps I wasn't what he thought I was going to be. Maybe I look nothing like my profile picture and maybe I'm not half as interesting as I seemed online. Maybe I'm an awful kisser. I wince at the memory of his lips on mine. We'd only met for a few hours. It's the cruelness of it all that really gets me. The indifference to my feelings.

He could have made his excuses and left but instead he waited until after he had kissed me and I had gone to the loo. He led me on and made me think the date was going okay. Great, even. Obviously not for him.

The rain is falling fast and heavy now and I sit here letting it drench me, washing away my tears, sending me into the depths of despair. Another wave of humiliation hits and it makes me think of *him*. Nick. And what he did to me. Ghosting, that's what they call it, and it's happened again. What's wrong with me? Why does this keep happening to me?

Denise arrives and I make my way over and hover a few feet from the bar as she pulls into the car park. My clothes are wet through, I shuffle to the car. She looks at my face and then at my clothes and looks horrified.

'What's happened?' The look of concern on her face and the kindness in her eyes are so strong that it sets me off again.

Now I'm sobbing and the rain dripping off me matches my tears. I can't get my words out. I can't explain. I can feel my shoulders involuntarily heaving up and down as I try to splutter it out.

'Hhee… lleeftt,' is all I manage but I'm not even sure who I'm talking about anymore, Lewis or Nick. I shiver, the cold searing into my bones freezing me to the core. It's the kind of cold that will take days to thaw.

'Oh sweetheart,' Denise says. 'We'll be back at yours in a minute, don't worry. Just try to breathe and get dry. There's a jumper on the back seat you can use to mop yourself up a bit.'

We travel the rest of the journey in silence. Denise occasionally rubs my shoulder and I try my hardest to get my tears under control and dry myself off. I feel stupid for being so upset when we've only just met.

I glance at my watch as we arrive home and at 10.10pm I know my parents will still be up. Despite being larks, they're also quite the night owls. Hopefully Jenna will have gone. I just want to be alone.

I walk into the house and go straight up to my room with Denise on my heels. As I enter the room Sara and Jenna are there already, sitting on my bed. Denise must have messaged them before she came to get me. I know they're trying to be kind but this makes the sting of humiliation even worse.

There's some wine and chocolates on my bedside table. I stare at my friends, their earnest faces, and burst into a fresh set of tears. I'd thought they'd all dried up but here they are again. Jenna comes over and folds me into her arms and I stand there sobbing again for several minutes. It makes me remember when we were children and Jenna was my most favourite person in the whole world. I'd have told her anything, before we grew apart.

As I calm down, I start to peel my dress off. I need comfort, I need my pyjamas and dressing gown. I still feel so cold inside and out.

I finally explain the humiliation to the girls and they all look horrified and I have to repeat several times that nothing else happened, that he just left when I went to the loo. The grass stains and mud on the back of my dress had been quite the cause for concern.

'That absolute arsehole! I thought there was something shifty about him,' Sara exclaims pushing a chocolate into her mouth.

'Why didn't you tell *me* then? I thought you said he looked nice,' I whine. Since when did he look shifty? Typical Sara to see something now that wasn't there then.

I look at the girls. 'Is it me? Is there something wrong with me? Why do men keep ghosting me? Maybe I'm a terrible kisser!'

Jenna looks between me, Denise and Sara. 'What is ghosting and who else has done this to you? Have you been left in a bar before?'

'Nick?' Denise questions and I nod quietly.

'Oh, not that wanker again. I thought you were over him. You've not mentioned him in ages,' Sara groans.

It took me a long time to get over Nick. Sara was clearly so sick of hearing me cry about him that I started to internalise it and resolved never to mention his name again, but he was always in the back of my mind.

Jenna looks puzzled. 'Nick? Nick, from the ship? But I thought it just fizzled out. That was what you said.' The look of realisation hits her face and I can see her working it all out. That's when our relationship really went downhill. I couldn't bear to look at her perfect little life, her wonderful husband and kids, while my life was such a mess. 'Oh God, Alma, why didn't you say anything?' Jenna looks aghast.

'Why do you think, it was so embarrassing. I was ashamed, I didn't want everyone to know. I thought I had a future with Nick but then he gets off the ship and

I never hear from him again. I never saw it coming. We had plans. I still don't understand it now. It's really messed with my head and now this has happened. So it must be me. What's wrong with me?' I wail.

'Aw it's not you, hun.' Denise comes over and rubs my back while handing me a fresh tissue to wipe my face.

'No, it's not you it's them. Give me your phone, I'll give that Lewis a what for!' Sara has gradually been looking more and more furious as the conversation has gone on. I'm really glad I deleted the app and his phone number now or she would be leaving hundreds of voice messages and texts on his phone.

'I've deleted the app and his number and blocked him so we can't contact him.' I think I've suffered enough for one night.

'Oh but...'

'No, Sara. I don't want to speak to him. He couldn't even be bothered to finish the night off or say goodbye. He'd just ignore my texts and add to my humiliation further. What if he left like that because I'm so ugly and horrible?' I put my face in my hands. I hope this is enough to stop Sara and she doesn't make her own *meant2b* account to hunt him down.

All the girls start to protest but I just wave my hands to signal that the discussion is over.

'Right, well, we've got bigger fish to fry really,' Sara starts.

'What are you talking about?' I'm so tired from the conversations I'm ready for everyone to leave now.

'Nick, let's find out why he did it. Yes, Lewis is a spineless weasel but what Nick did to you was worse. He was in a relationship with you. I want to talk to him.' I can see the determination in her eyes and I know that I'm going to be fighting a losing battle over this.

This evening has gone from bad to worse.

'I don't even know his address. He lives a few hours away in Linkley but that's all I know. We'll never find him. There's no point in trying,' I say, attempting to stop the situation from going any further. What if Sara does find Nick?

With that Denise's eyes light up. 'What's his surname again? I remember it's a bit of a weird one. I've watched lots of episodes of *Catfish*, I bet I could find him. Do you have an email address? Where's your laptop? Does he have social media?'

'Okay, well we can look, but we'll probably not find him. He always prided himself on not being on social media. It was his thing and it was kind of annoying actually, the way he went on about it, so we won't find him online easily. It's Nick Jones-Silvine.' It surely can't be that easy to find someone. This is ridiculous but at least it's a distraction from tonight's disaster.

I pull up my laptop and we all crowd round. Denise starts to work her magic, she really is in her element typing in his name and area, email address and any other tiny droplets of information I can give her. It takes only moments before she finds a Jane and Donald Jones- Silvine on a website she has to sign into – she's obviously done this before. They're his parents, there's no phone number but we now have an address. I'm relieved, even though we're not going to drive up there and turn up at his parents' door.

That would be crazy, wouldn't it?

'Let's go up there and find out why he did it. Let's tell him off so he never does it again. Why does he think he can get away with this? You need this, you need closure, Alma.' Sara's eyes shine with excitement at the formation of a plan.

'We could, you know,' Denise says slowly, trying to gauge my reaction.

Oh, Denise, not you too I thought you'd be on my side.

'You need the closure. This has affected you for far too long,' she says by way of explanation. 'I'm on half term so we could go up tomorrow? Sara you choose your hours so you're okay. What about you, Alma?'

'No, no way. I can't get the time off work. I've got an important meeting tomorrow,' I protest. In all honesty I'm dreading the next week at work. We have a big meeting tomorrow and then I'm spending the rest of the week training two new members of staff on our inhouse system. It wouldn't be so bad but I don't even get paid for the pleasure. To add insult to injury they are both my superiors and younger than me.

'Pull a sickie,' Jenna says and I'm shocked at her for this. She was always so conscientious, even though she doesn't work and hasn't since she had the kids, she would never have missed a day's work for something so frivolous.

'I can't. My boss is a real stickler for people who pull sickies on a Monday. Never believes them anyway. I almost ended up in a disciplinary hearing last time I had the flu that landed on a Monday. So unless I'm dying, I always go in, even if it's only so they can see I'm dying.'

They all roll their eyes; they think I'm being dramatic but they don't know what Liz, my boss, is like.

'Well, go in tomorrow and pretend to feel ill. Take some pills in and a packet of tissues, pop them on your desk, talk with a croaky voice, Bob's your uncle,' Denise adds. I'm seeing a dark side to Denise. I always thought she was so sweet and innocent, teaching tiny children. I'm beginning to wonder now.

I can see that I'm not going to get anywhere with them. I decide to take the path of least resistance and agree. The truth is it would be good to get some closure from Nick. I would like to know why he made all those plans with me and then left me without so much as a text. I've kept all of the shame and pain from Nick deep down and this horrible date with Lewis has brought it back to the surface. Perhaps knowing would help me to move on properly. Perhaps it's what has stopped me before, I reluctantly admit to myself.

Maybe Lewis felt I was still broken when he kissed me and that's why he ran a mile. I've not felt good about myself in a long time, maybe this would be a great way of me regaining control of my life. Why am I giving these men so much power over me? The girls are right; Nick doesn't deserve to get away with this. He never saw how he affected me. He just got to get off the ship and forget all about me. He stole our breakup from me. I never got to scream and shout. I never got to ask why. Well, it may be a year later but Nick Jones-Silvine we're coming to get you.

'Looks like we're going to Linkley then,' I say.

Chapter 6

1 year earlier

'Wow, talk about leaving it to the last minute,' Kelly says examining my cabin. It's a lot smaller than what she's used to. Photographers don't get as much room as the 'talent'. A shared cabin with bunk beds and just enough cupboard space for two is all we get, whereas she gets a whole cabin to herself. Cramped is an understatement but I've thanked my lucky stars that the cabin is above sea level and with a small porthole. It could be worse, a lot worse. Some of the cabin stewards and waiters are four to a cabin and below sea level, which means no natural light. It may be great for sleeping at any time during the day but not so good for your mental health.

'I know, I know, I'm almost done.' I pick up a load of clothes draped on a chair and proceed to stuff them into my suitcase as quickly as possible. I'm so excited to be getting off the ship but I'm also really nervous. There're so many thoughts going around in my head that it's spinning.

'Okay, tell the floor that when you see it.' Kelly

laughs and tosses her long blonde hair back, showing off her tanned shoulders.

'Are you all ready?' I ask, already knowing the answer.

'Yep, packed yesterday, we weren't performing so it was a pretty chilled day and we all went out for dinner.' She means they went to one of the intimate restaurants, the ones you have to pay for.

Pursing my lips, I swallow back my jealousy; I'd barely left the photo gallery by midnight and I've only just finished the morning shift. My God, I need a break. Eight months on board is enough to drive anyone crazy, never mind the long sixty/seventy plus hour weeks with barely a day off. Ship life is a mixture of extreme highs and lows, from filming on the docks of the Panama canal, standing at the top of Christ the Redeemer and trekking the waterfalls in St Vincent to being yelled at and humiliated in the restaurant by an old man who doesn't want a soft focus portrait or to be disturbed during dinner. Leaving the restaurant with silent tears sliding down your face and the rest of the evening left to work.

I've had an extreme time. I'm happy to move on but I know I will miss it too. Ship life is its own little bubble; working with, living with and socialising with the same people. We've grown amazing bonds and friendships, though some have also grown enemies. Kelly is one of my best friends now. It seems mad that a mere six months ago we didn't even know each other. We've grown really close and I am going to miss her like hell. Kelly has another contract as a dancer on one of the Australian cruise ships.

A small part of me feels jealous but I am ready to move on with Nick and I'm excited to see what the future brings for us. At the thought of Nick, I check my phone for what feels like the hundredth time. Why isn't he responding to me? A feeling of dread engulfs me and I'm feeling unsure about a future I was so looking forward to a mere two weeks ago. Everything has been fine between us so I don't understand why he's suddenly gone AWOL.

'What do you think is up with Nick?' I ask Kelly. As my BFF on board and a friend of Nick's she knows us both well so I hope she has some insight.

'Maybe he's lost his phone or something?' she guesses. 'I wouldn't worry, I'm sure it's all fine. Have you sorted something out in case he isn't there?' she asks, broaching the subject softly. I know she's just being a good friend but that's the last thing I want to hear. I'm sure he's going to be there, the last time we saw each other was great. We were as much in love as ever.

I can feel the bile rise up in my chest at the idea of Nick not turning up; it's ludicrous, we were attached at the hip. Always together. Why wouldn't he turn up? Kelly's right he probably has just lost his phone and I bet he has been so busy catching up with all of his friends he's barely had a minute to do anything about it. It's not like anyone else on board has heard from him. I asked all of his friends and he doesn't have social media so there's no way of finding him on Facebook or Instagram. That's always been something he's been proud of but in this instance it's incredibly irritating, at the very least other people would be tagging him in places and I'd know he was safe and well.

'There's a bus I can get, it'll be fine,' I say. 'Or I could get my parents to come. Who's picking you up?' I play it down.

In reality I will definitely not be asking my parents to come down to pick me up. It would be too mortifying. After all, they're expecting me and Nick to turn up together. They're expecting to meet him. If he isn't here, I'm going to have to spend the long and horrible journey home working out what to say to them and how to do it without breaking down into tears of shame. I've told everyone about this amazing guy I've met. I've told them about our plans. This is my first and last contract on the ship, while I enjoyed it, we decided to give it a shot in the real world; get *normal* jobs and live together. I've already let the photography department know I won't be coming back; I can't change my mind now. Imagine having to tell everyone on board if he doesn't turn up. I could never live it down.

'My Dad's picking me up, he's always late so I'm in no hurry,' Kelly says rolling her eyes.

'I'm nearly done. Shall we get our stuff off and go see if Nick is in the terminal?' I'm grateful for Kelly's support. If he doesn't turn up, I might just need her.

'Sure, I'll meet you on the gangway in ten? Have you got everything?'

'Yes, and yes. Okay, I'll see you in ten.' I force a smile.

I take down the last of my photos, the ones stuck up by my bunk. I look longingly at the images of Nick and me. There's a whole selection of photos of us in Rome, I remember how badly my feet ached after that day having walked all over the city together. We took in the amazing sights of the Trevi Fountain, throwing in our coins and making our wishes, we visited St Peter's Square and the Colosseum. It was the perfect date, we walked and talked non-stop. I was so happy that day.

That was the day we made it official. Boyfriend and girlfriend.

Images of us in Copenhagen bring back such sweet memories. We went to the markets, holding hands the whole day, trying our first bratwurst and laughing uncontrollably about it.

I remember the first time that I saw Nick. So handsome and self-assured, I was instantly attracted to him. He was one of the singers in the shows, it seemed to me like all the girls were mesmerised by him and I felt so lucky when he picked me. I just don't understand it. Please be there. Nick. Please show up. Why aren't you speaking to me? What's wrong?

Three hours later and I'm beginning to lose hope. Kelly's Dad is running really late, stuck in some horrendous traffic or something and she has kindly sat with me for the past few hours but I know he'll get here soon and she's getting impatient.

'I'd offer you a ride but you're in the opposite direction, aren't you?' she says kindly. I wish the floor would just swallow me up right now; the longer I wait the clearer it is.

'Yes,' I say quietly putting my head in my hands. I can't believe he isn't here. When he stopped responding I didn't understand it and I don't understand this. Why is he doing this? Why won't he tell me what's going on. I hope he is okay. What if something has happened to him? I don't know whether to be angry or sad. My heart is breaking.

Kelly rubs my shoulder soothingly. 'I know it doesn't feel like it right now, but it will be okay,' she says. I look up at her, appreciating the reassurance. 'Why don't you call your mum, I can do it if you like?' she offers.

'No, it's okay, I think I'll catch the bus,' I say trying to wipe away my tears and put a brave face on it.

We both sit there quietly whilst my heart breaks. While we've been waiting, we've seen lots of our friends and staff members getting off the ship and saying their farewells. It's getting to the last few stragglers coming off the ship now and I'm pleased I won't have to pretend that Nick's been held up and everything is fine to anyone else asking.

'Hello, what are you still doing here?' John, another of the singers, interrupts my train of thought and I roll my eyes internally, another person to pretend to.

'Just waiting on Nick. He should be here soon,' I say, hoping that'll be the end of it.

'Oh really, he never mentioned he was in Southampton today,' he says looking at his phone.

'You've spoken to him?' I ask puzzled. So, someone has heard from him. How did I not know this? I asked around but I didn't want to rouse too much suspicion but I really thought no one had heard from him.

'Oh yes, just today. Sounds like he's having an amazing time at home. I've got to go anyway, my family's here.' He gestures towards the double doors and jogs out of the terminal.

I am flabbergasted. So, his phone is working. Nick is just ignoring me. He's ghosting me. The realisation stings like a slap in the face. I can hardly breathe. I start to sob uncontrollably and make my way to the toilets to hide away. I don't want to see anyone. Or anyone to see me.

'What a fucking wanker,' Kelly mutters as she enters

the toilets.

'I know. I can't believe it,' I sob. I don't have the heart to talk about it anymore. I just want to go home and hide away in my room.

'I'll walk you to the bus stop,' Kelly says, putting her arm around me. I feel heavy with sorrow.

'You don't need to, isn't your Dad nearly here,' I whine, but I know she's already coming with me, even if she has to make her Dad wait and I'm grateful for that.

Kelly looks at her phone and sends off a message and receives a speedy reply. 'No, he'll be about half an hour.'

We get up and walk in silence to the bus stop and I brush away the silent tears that won't stop coming. I'll need to catch the crew bus into the town centre and then, if I'm lucky I'll be able to get on a direct bus straight to my home town, but it'll still take over four hours. It's going to be a long and sad journey and I'm already dreading it. I don't know that the full weight of what has happened has hit me yet. Nick didn't turn up for me. He left me here. He has been speaking to other people on board. He didn't lose his phone. He's fine. He's happy. He's having an amazing time.

'Thanks for waiting with me,' I sniffle.

'I know it sucks right now but it will get better. You'll be fine.' Kelly rubs my shoulder, trying to soothe me but it's no use. My worst fears have manifested.

'I know,' I say, but I don't know because my world has just been ripped from underneath me and I don't know what to believe anymore.

I'm crushed. I'm numb. I sit on the bus crying all the way home.

Chapter 7

Now

I drag myself out of bed early the next morning. My head is banging and whirling from the events of last night. I risk a glance in my full-length mirror. I am a state, my eyes are puffy from all the crying and the once lovely soft waves have turned to frizz from all the rain. I pull my hair up into my usual bun and put some eye drops in. I really look like crap, perhaps getting out of work won't be so difficult after all. I wander downstairs to see Mum sitting at the kitchen island with an empty cup of tea in front of her. It's clear to me she's been sat here waiting for me to come down.

'Everything alright love? There was a lot going on last night? I think everyone left when I was going to bed.' She giggles nervously as she takes in my haggard appearance.

She knows that the date was awful, she'd have been in my room saying it was too late and everyone needed to leave otherwise. I wonder what Jenna told her. I wish I wasn't still living at home; it really makes me feel I'm under a microscope.

I love my mum, she's so kind and warm, but since she retired, she's forever milling around the house. We get under each other's feet constantly. I bet at sixty-eight she thought all of her children would have flown the nest and she'd be able to enjoy her twilight years with grandchildren and freedom. She deserves to have some peace; I feel instantly guilty for failing her. She looks so tired and I can see that she doesn't want to push too hard but she is worried about me. Mum thought she would never have children, just one of those things the doctors told her, so Jenna was her miracle baby. They never really expected to have a second baby especially when Mum was in her forties but they couldn't look a gift horse in the mouth and she always tells everyone how fortunate they were to have me too.

'Yes, I'm fine, date didn't go too well that's all. Nothing big,' I say, downplaying it. 'Anyway, onwards and upwards. I'm going to make a pot of tea. Would you like some?' I give her empty cup a meaningful look. Hopefully we won't need to talk about *my date* any further. Tea solves everything after all.

'Yes, that would be lovely.' Mum smiles.

Dad ambles in, a man of few words but always there. He comes over and places a hand on my shoulder and smiles, it's such a small gesture but I know he knows. I know he cares and I appreciate it. I can see why Mum and Dad have been happily married for so long. I wish that I had a relationship like theirs. By my age they'd already been married for years.

'Toast for anyone?' he asks. And like that he drops his hand and the moment evaporates as if it never was.

I grab a quick piece of toast and down two cups of tea to wake me up. I have a good rummage in the drug drawer but all I can find is a packet of gum, plasters, bandages, multivitamins and a box of Imodium Instants – which provide on-the-go relief for diarrhoea, apparently. I idly wonder who these belong to. Yuck. I grab a packet of tissues and take the Imodium with me; it will have to do. I could really have done with some paracetamol right now. To avoid Mum and Dad's questioning looks I leave for work uncharacteristically early, pretending I have important work to do that just can't wait.

♥♥♥

The office is very quiet at 7.30am. The only person in apart from me is my manager Liz. Liz is generally lovely, although a bit of a busybody and a micromanager. Over the year I have gained her trust and she now knows I can be reliably left to my own devices, but it's taken a lot of hours with her looking over my shoulder to get it.

Liz is also a huge germaphobe. We've recently moved to hot-desking to allow for the too many staff to desk ratio. Our superiors all take it in turns to homework for one day a week to allow the rest of us 'inferiors' to fit in the office. It's Liz's worse nightmare and although she would never admit it, we all know she comes in at seven every day to clean her desk and ensure she doesn't actually have to hot desk. The hot desks work on a first come, first serve basis.

I take a seat near the window on the opposite side of the office. If I'm in I want to take advantage and get as much work done as possible. I've also carefully chosen a seat where I'll need to walk past Liz on my many planned trips to the toilet. I've got to sell it after all.

Liz is hard at work with her antibacterial wipes giving the desk a good going over, her arm working so fast it looks like a real workout to me. Perhaps that's the secret of her waif like figure and lank hair, she often looks very pale and sickly. If she scrubs herself that vigorously too it's no wonder. After finishing up she looks around the office and does a double take at me. Okay, I admit it, I'm never in the office early. I usually start late and stay late. I know this will have rattled her, routine is her best friend and I'm messing with it.

Liz walks over to my desk, shimmying in her pencil skirt as she heads towards me. Solemnly squirting her hands with sanitizer, she rubs them together vigorously. She does this a lot, so often in fact that it's like a nervous tick; I often wonder if she's even aware of it.

'Hi Alma, you're in early. I don't think I've *ever* seen you in so early.' She runs her eyes over me and my desk and spots the Imodium and tissues strategically placed.

I take a sip of my water, and then gulp it back. My hair, despite being frizzy, is also greasy from all Jenna's styling last night, and everyone knows unkempt hair is a sign of illness, just watch any soap. I'd have normally spent the morning lying in bed then washing my hair. I doubt I would have made it in before 10am. Thank God for flexible working, that is one of the few perks of my job.

'I'm not feeling too great so just wanted to get in and get on with everything. Couldn't sleep,' I croak. I can tell Liz is already itching to leave, she can probably feel the germs invading her body as we speak but she'd hate to be rude.

'Are you sure you should be in?' Liz takes a good look at me now, taking in my puffy eyes. I've not worn any make-up today so I know it's only a matter of time before someone tells me I look peaky. Yet more evidence that I'm ill.

'I'm fine. I'll muddle through,' I say. What a hero I am even though I'm so unwell I've still come in, surely this will get me some brownie points around the office. I offer her a small smile. 'We have that important meeting and training this week.' Aren't I just the model employee? Little does Liz know I won't be muddling through tomorrow.

Liz nods her head. 'Well, if you're sure. Let me know if you need to go home.' She hurries back to her desk. She can barely stand being near my germs another second. As she walks away, I see her pull out the hand sanitizer from her jacket pocket and go through the motion of rubbing her hands all over again. They must be red raw.

A few hours later and I have walked back and forth to the toilet three times. This is the fourth time I'm going. The office is really filling up now. I've had two people tell me I look peaky and most people are opting to sit on the opposite side of the office. Is it something I said?

There are two unisex toilets at work. They changed them from separate men's and women's to 'get with the times' and it caused a real uproar across the staff. I don't tend to care that much but I know what they mean. I don't particularly want to touch a wet toilet seat or stand in wee for that matter. I know I shouldn't generalise, but a lot of men are not good at aiming, and they sprinkle.

As I turn around the corner, I walk past Steve from

HR. He's coming from the loos and is in a bit of a hurry. Probably keen to get back to that dirty kebab I saw him scoffing at his desk earlier. Who has kebab for breakfast? Disgusting. It's the kind of thing you have at the end of a boozy night out. Well into his fifties I can't imagine Steve has many of those anymore and certainly not on a Sunday night.

One of the toilets is out of order so the other one is in high demand today, especially with my many trips. There's no one here now except me so I go straight in. Oh my God, I now understand why Steve was in such a hurry. It stinks. It's so disgusting I can feel my eyes smarting. I'm not sure what to do. I suddenly wish I could have Liz's hand sanitizer to bathe in. I only came to the loo to make it look like I had a stomach bug. I think something dead came out of Steve's arse. That's it. I'm just going to leave, otherwise I *will* be calling in sick, but for real.

I step out of the toilet and while I've been gone a small queue has formed; how has there even been time? These poor bastards don't know what's coming. Right at the front of the queue is Liz. I'm horrified, she's going to think that stink is me, that I did that. Well if I wanted her to think that I was ill I've done an excellent job now. Thanks a lot, kebab Steve. This is going to floor poor Liz.

I hurry away from the toilets; I know just how Steve felt except it wasn't me who made that gut-wrenching stench. I sit back at my desk and try not to think about it. I mean she's not going to say anything to me, is she? It's not like I'd go to Steve and tell him whatever he did stank like a dead skunk.

Twenty minutes later and I'm tap-tapping on my computer when Liz and Steve approach me. I look up puzzled; why are they here? Liz has her hand sanitizer and is already slathering it all over herself, her sleeves are rolled up and she's really going for it. After that smell I'm not surprised, she's looking a bit peaky herself.

'Can we have a word?' Steve asks.

Are they going to talk to me about that stink? Surely not, especially when Steve knows it was really him. I can feel my cheeks begin to colour. Maybe it's not about that at all. Do they know I'm pretending? How would they? I can't think why HR would be over here with my manager. Steve and Liz lead me over to the HR room. I can feel myself begin to sweat, am I going to be sacked? I mentally go over all my recent work and try and think if I've done anything wrong or that I'd be in trouble for but nothing comes to mind.

Steve clears his throat uncomfortably. 'We've called this meeting because we're just a bit concerned about you. How are you?'

What do I say? Lie, of course, what else can I do? 'Um, well, not too good really.'

'That's what we thought. I need to remind you about the policy around sickness and diarrhoea.'

Steve goes on to regale me on why we should not be in the office if we have these illnesses and that it's irresponsible to be spreading them around and that we shouldn't be here for forty-eight hours after an 'episode'. Liz's face goes from white to green, and, uncharacteristically, she leaves all the talking to Steve. After that smell she must be feeling pretty sick herself. I want to scream that it wasn't me. I want to point the finger at Steve and his dirty kebab habit, and tell Liz that he's the culprit. I hate that she is always going to associate that stench with me.

What a hypocrite Steve is. There's definitely something wrong with his bowels and he is still here. I nod along feeling more and more embarrassed. Why didn't I just call in sick this morning? It would have been so much easier or I should have gone home earlier. Trying to finish off my work has seriously backfired and now Liz thinks I'm disgusting. She may never be able to look at me again. She's hand-sanitized three times whilst we've been talking, at this rate she'll have no skin left.

'So, considering all of this, we think you should go home for the day and I don't expect to see you back in the office before Thursday or later. Remember only after forty-eight hours have passed and an episode has not occurred can you return. Keep in touch with Liz and let us know how you are. Get well soon.'

Liz nods along. 'I hope you're feeling better soon. Shall we stay and have a chat about any outstanding work I need to take on?'

I nod my agreement, although I cannot look her in the eye.

'Well, I'll leave you ladies to it.' Steve gets up to leave but not before leaving us a little present. Safe in the knowledge that Liz will think it's me he has let off another stinker and it smells worse than in the toilets. I want to gag.

Liz puts her hand to her mouth and can't hide her disgust. Ever the professional she doesn't say anything about the smell but her eyes flick to the window. I think she's deciding how rude it would be to go and open it, because then she'd be admitting to smelling *my* stink. If I go and open it then I'm admitting that *I* did it. It's a standoff, neither of us wants to go over and make it obvious, but the stench is rancid. Steve is getting away scot-free leaving his stink in his wake and framing me for it. Steve I won't forget this, you can be sure of that.

'On second thoughts, why don't you just send over any bits via email? There can't be much, can there?' she asks, allowing us both to escape the room and Steve's stink.

I go back to my desk and quickly and quietly send over the few pieces of work that need to be done in the next few days. I also take the Imodium off my desk and hide it away. I feel really embarrassed but I'm also secretly pleased I'm about to go home and it's only twelve. I've also gained at least half of the week off work. I suppose things could be worse. I look over at Liz, she's still green. I bet she won't be eating for the rest of the day.

Perhaps she'll be heading home with my 'bug' too.

Chapter 8

'That's hilarious, so Steve shitty pants framed you.' I hold the phone away from my ear while Sara cackles loudly. 'Silver linings, whatever died up his arse got you out of work. This is great, have you told the others? Why don't we leave this afternoon? Nothing stopping us now.'

'Hmmm, I know I said we would but I'm really not sure if we should do this. I've been thinking about it, I don't think it's a good idea. I mean what's he going to say?' The more it's churned around in my head, the worse the idea seems. This surely won't end well.

Sara's tone turns serious. 'Nick really hurt you. Don't you think he should know what he did to you? Don't you think you deserve some answers as to why he did it? And most importantly you deserve the closure to finally move on. We're doing this and that's final,' she says with conviction. 'I'll call the others and we'll be over in about an hour. Get yourself packed and ready. Bring some stuff for a few nights. Also bring some nice clothes and we'll go out on the town. We want him to see what he's missing after all.'

I groan inwardly. 'But we've already established I don't have anything nice.' I fall back onto my bed, thinking about last night and the girls ripping apart of my wardrobe.

'Okay, okay, calm down. I'll bring something, anyway I'm going now. Things to sort. See you soon. Be ready.' With that Sara ends the call, not one to worry about pleasantries.

♥♥♥

An hour later and I've packed as if I'm going abroad for a week's holiday. I've piled in lots of make-up and clothes for every and any occasion. I've even packed a swimming costume, in case I bump into him at a pool? I think not. Jenna pulls up in her blue Ford Kuga and beeps the horn.

Dad sticks his head round my bedroom door. 'Love I think your ride's here. Going anywhere nice?'

'Oh, just for a few days away with the girls, got a few days off work,' I offer as explanation. True to his usual style he doesn't ask anything further, satisfied with my original answer he heads back downstairs, presumably to report to Mum. I know she won't be pleased with the lack of detail; she's dying to know why I came home at 12 and now I'm going back out. Her head must be spinning. I fly downstairs and out of the door as quickly as possible so she can't intercept me.

I appraise Jenna's car; she's forever chauffeuring around my niece and nephew and I can see they've left their stamp. I didn't fully realise she'd be coming on this trip and I feel bad that if I'd done the phoning round, I wouldn't have called her.

'Sorry about the mess, I thought we were going

tomorrow but this will have to do. I'd have got Sam and Claire to tidy it up otherwise,' says Jenna, rolling her eyes. It occurs to me that she could tidy it up herself but I can tell it's not her mess, so fair enough and she's doing us all a favour by driving, so I don't say anything.

'Hey, everyone.' Jenna has already picked up the others. Sara has bagged herself the front seat and Denise is in the back behind Jenna. I heave my bags in the boot and in comparison to Sara I have packed quite frugally. No surprises there. There's a large leopard print case and a matching carry-on version. I can also see one other small carry-on bag which I guess is Denise's and looks the most appropriate size, considering the trip we are going on.

'Jenna, where are your bags?' I ask searching in the back.

'Oh I don't need much, there's a bag behind Sara's.' I finally spot a small shoulder bag at the back. Now there's frugality.

I climb in trying to step over all the sweet wrappers and crisp packets and general mess in the footwell but end up with my feet on top of something lumpy. I pick it up and as I do a sock falls out. A sweaty stench is released. This is definitely not a fresh sock. I wish I had Liz's sanitizer now, urgh, I feel sick. Again. I've had enough of smells today. I consider feigning sickness to get out of *this* trip. If I say it now, it won't even be a lie. I don't think any of them would go for it though. Jenna spies my horrified face.

'That's Sam's, sorry.' She moves her hand as if to dismiss it. I see Denise and Sara make faces as the odour spreads through the car. Never one for subtlety, Sara rolls down her window and sticks her head out.

My fifteen-year-old nephew is disgusting. I'll remember this, Sam. Jenna doesn't even flinch, these smells must be the norm for her. I bet his room absolutely reeks if this is the effect of just one sock.

I quickly shove the stinking sock back into the bag and push it as far forward under the seat in front as I can. I really hope the smell doesn't linger.

'Who's looking after Sam and Claire whilst you're away?' I ask Jenna. Normally she's barely separated from her perfect family so I find it strange she's agreed to go on this trip.

'Well, they are teenagers, and Dave is around. They don't need me so much now,' she says, turning the music up to signal the end of the conversation. I guess since she's having a few days away from the kids she really wants to enjoy it, fair enough. We will definitely have to make sure we make time for a night out. I can't remember the last time I went out with Jenna. Perhaps this trip won't be so bad.

Linkley is a three-hour drive from Twinton. Jenna has planned everything down to the last detail including which services we'll stop at and where we are going to stay; a Travel Lodge in the centre and a fifteen-minute drive from Nick's parents' place. Trust Jenna to take over when I don't think she should even be here. I try to push my annoyance down and remember this is supposed to be a bit of fun and me getting closure.

Ninety minutes into the journey and we've reached our designated stopping area. I requested a stop at the one twenty minutes ago to go to the loo but Jenna had gone on and on about the plan so much that I gave in and agreed to wait the extra twenty minutes. I am now bursting and head straight for the loos the minute we get out of the car. We agree to meet in the shop afterwards to get some drinks and snacks for the rest of the drive. In my haste to avoid Mum when I left, I've not even had lunch.

As I come into the shop, I see *him*. It's so unexpected I don't exactly know what to do with myself, he's standing in the queue waiting patiently. I've entered the shop now so I don't want to draw attention to myself by walking straight out, even if that's exactly what I want to do. He definitely hasn't seen me so that's a small mercy. I head down one of the aisles. Unlike me he's pretty tall so he may be able to see me over the aisles. Determined that he won't see me I sit down on the floor; I'm going to sit here until he leaves. I see Denise enter the shop. She turns into the aisle I'm in all the while staring at me with a baffled expression.

'What are you doing?' she asks, her voice far too loud. Denise isn't known for being loud, typical that when I'm trying to hide, she has suddenly found her biggest voice.

'Shhh, sit down. Lewis is here,' I hiss, tugging at her skirt to get her to be less conspicuous.

Realisation dawns on her face. 'Lewis the Loo Loser?' she asks, her head swishing this way and that to get a good look. I tug at her again and she finally sits down.

'Yes.' I can feel the heat start to colour my cheeks. I thought I'd never see him again. Why here. Why now? Could this trip get any worse?

'What's he doing here?' Denise asks.

'How the hell do I know?'

'Okay, well why are we sat on the floor?' Denise

gestures around us with a puzzled expression.

'Because we're already on a crazy mission to confront one man and I don't have the energy to do two.' I'm mortified and I really hope Sara doesn't spot us because she will probably go over and give him a good talking to. I can see him at the tills now chatting and smiling away with the girl on the checkout who's smiling back at him, almost flirting. Little does she know that he's an arsehole. Don't be fooled. He turns to leave and I hope I've managed to get away with hiding. I'm keen to leave as quickly as possible just in case we bump into him again. If I can just get the girls into the car now, I won't ever have to see Lewis the Loo Loser again. What is he doing here?

Sara and Jenna come around the aisle and nearly fall over us.

'What are you two weirdos doing on the floor?' Jenna asks putting her hand out to help me up.

I look pleadingly at Denise. I really don't want them to convince me to confront him.

'Just looking at the sweets down here,' she says motioning to the treats in front of us. I'm so glad we stopped in this aisle and not the one full of car tow ropes and antifreeze.

'Okay.' Sara shrugs. 'Well you both probably didn't need to sit down. Anyway, hurry up. There's an ice cream van outside and I want a double choc with flakes.'

'I think we should get on now. I'm not sure Jenna has allowed time for ice cream in her schedule.' I'm trying to appeal to Jenna's need for control and sticking to her plan. I'm sure she doesn't want us to mess with her expected time of arrival.

'You're right, but I suppose you could eat them in

the car. It is a travelling rubbish bin, you're lucky I haven't had a chance to clean it.' Jenna rolls her eyes.

Damn you, Sam and Claire. I'm going to get you both clothes for Christmas this year, that'll show you.

I suppose it won't take long to get ice creams but the sooner we can get out of here the better. I subtly look around but there's no Lewis in sight. Sara, Denise and I all queue at the van for our ice creams. Denise and I opt for a small whippy ice cream cone with strawberry sauce. Sara gets a large whippy chocolate ice cream cone with chocolate sprinkles and a flake. It is gargantuan. It's typical of Sara to get something so huge. She loves that people can never believe, looking at her slender figure, how much she eats. I can see Jenna eyeing Sara's ice cream. Her car may be a mess but I'm sure she doesn't want that all over it. She goes to open her mouth about to say something but uses her better judgement and closes it again. She's probably reminding herself that we are adults, not teenagers.

We clamber into the car, ice creams in hand and I finally feel like I can breathe. Thankfully Denise hasn't said anything about Lewis being there and now I can relax.

As we pull out of the car park Sara is the first to spot him standing on the other side of the road waiting to cross. His head is down checking something on his phone. He's wearing a shirt and jeans and as much as I hate to admit it, he looks rather good. What a wanker.

'I can't believe it. That guy looks just like Lewis,' she exclaims pointing towards him and bending forward to get a better look.

I watch the back of Sara's head, willing her to look away, and then I look pleadingly at Denise who purses her lips. Sara turns and looks at me and reads the expression on my face. She's very in tune with people's body language and anything I say now will be futile.

'Oh my God, it *is* him. Isn't it? Is that why you were sat on the floor? I knew something was going on.' She laughs and tilts her head back.

Denise gives me an apologetic look and readjusts her glasses.

Sara's ice cream has begun to melt and a large drop falls onto her lap, but even that can't distract Jenna. Her head is twisting around trying to get a good look as we crawl past. There are lots of cars zooming past on either side and he's waiting patiently to be let across to no avail. Jenna swerves slightly and we all gasp, clutching at our ice creams.

'Concentrate on the road,' I yell. 'Let's get out of here, never mind about *him*,' I say, trying to put an end to the torment.

'Turn around at the roundabout,' Sara commands, looking at Jenna.

'No. Don't,' I plead. 'I don't want to confront him.'

'Yes, let's just carry on,' Denise adds, trying to help.

'Who said anything about confronting him?' Sara asks with a wicked grin and a glint in her eye.

'I'm turning. I want to see what Sara has planned.' Jenna turns around at the mini roundabout just after the service station. Lewis is still standing at the kerb patiently and Jenna, under Sara's instructions, slows the car right down. The cars on the other side are going quite fast so Lewis is stuck at the side of the road. The cars behind us aren't too happy and a horn beeps to signal for us to move on. As this happens Lewis looks up, we're really close to him now and on the same side of the road, Sara rolls down her window and lobs her ice cream at him as hard as she can. It hits him square in the face.

I'm so shocked I sit there and stare while Denise and Sara duck. Without the foresight to duck my eyes lock with his. The double chocolate ice cream is sliding down his face and all over his clothes, the coverage is very impressive. I can't help but grin, the colour of the ice cream makes it look as though he's covered in shit. He has definitely seen me now. My heart is racing. He must think it was me. He deserves it though, the wanker. Jenna carries on down the road where there's another small roundabout ahead.

'Now he really looks like a loo loser,' Sara cackles and we all burst into fits of laughter.

'Shit face,' Jenna mutters.

Sara is rummaging around under the seat while Jenna turns the car back around to continue on our journey. I can see him walking back towards the services, presumably to go to the toilets. He needs a good cleaning up now. I almost feel sorry for him.

'Ah-ha,' Sara exclaims sitting up straight. She rolls down her window again and lobs the stinking sock out the window. It catches him on the back of the head. He turns and I can see he is absolutely fuming now. The sock has set off a fresh bout of giggles and everyone is doing big belly laughs. Now that was fun.

Throughout the rest of the journey whenever there's a little bit of silence, someone says ice cream or sock and it sets us all off again. I haven't laughed so much in a very long time. Perhaps this trip was a good idea after all. I feel quite elated after that. We got Lewis and he's had his just desserts.

Now we're coming for you, Nick.

Chapter 9

We arrive at the Travel Lodge around 5pm. The rest of the car journey was filled with fun, still on a high from the ice cream-sock-Lewis incident and full of sugar we sung at the tops of our lungs and laughed all the way here.

My mood dissipates a little when we check into our room. Jenna has booked a room with two double beds so it's like going away for a huge sleepover. I'm not sure why we couldn't have had our own rooms or perhaps two separate rooms but I'll have to make the most of it. As Jenna is my sister, I opt to share a bed with her. I hope she doesn't snore like she did when we were kids. I feel a bit irritated that she didn't even consult us over the room booking, she just can't help but take over the trip. Denise and Sara may not have wanted to share a bed, especially if Sara wants to bring someone back. I clench my jaw, they're too kind to say anything, so I resolve to shrug it off and let it go.

We all agree that we won't go and search out Nick tonight. I'm really relieved as I want to get my wits about me before the dreaded confrontation. Instead we decide to go out for a low-key dinner and I cross my fingers that we don't bump into him. Linkely can't be that small surely? And what are the chances of bumping into him after the Lewis bumping into situation? Highly unlikely.

♥♥♥

'What the hell is all that?' Jenna's face is a picture.

After dragging it all the way up to the room Sara has just opened her small suitcase to reveal that she's basically packed a bar into it. There are all sorts; wine, spirits and even mixers, it's pretty impressive to be honest.

'Well, I thought we shouldn't waste time going to the supermarket and we may all need a few drinks. Especially this one,' she says, giving me a squeeze. 'Come on, what does everyone want?' She pulls out a pack of plastic glasses, this girl thinks of everything.

I opt for the wine to stay on the safe side. I don't want to mix my drinks and have a dirty hangover in the morning. Sara expertly pours everyone a glass. Denise and Jenna both have vodka and cokes, and Sara makes herself a Sex on the Beach, she's even packed a cocktail shaker.

Next, she opens up her large bag and inside is an array of clothes for all occasions. I spot a swimming costume in her bag and grin to myself, looks like I'm not the only one who's over prepared.

'Help yourself, Alma,' she says. I go and tentatively have a look remembering the clothes she brought over for my date with the loo loser and hope that it's not that same selection again. The green dress, which is wasting away at the bottom of my laundry basket, is the

66

only thing I would wear and feel comfortable in. But this time there's a different assortment and some of them are really nice, a bit more daring than I'd normally go for but I could definitely wear some of these. Things are looking up again.

'Thanks, Sara, that's really sweet of you.'

'Jenna, Denise help yourselves too if you want to borrow anything, go for it.'

Oh no, now I've got to fight the others for the best clothes. I start to rummage quickly to ensure I get the outfit I want and don't pine after what someone else is wearing all evening. I settle on a tight black dress that comes down to my knee, with flowers up the side. I keep glancing at myself in the mirror, I do look quite good actually. Maybe I do need to rethink my wardrobe after all, my own clothes never make me feel like this. Maybe they are a bit drab.

'Let me do your make-up this time, Alma?' Sara asks, looking at me warily.

'Um, sure.' I don't want to offend her when she's brought all these lovely clothes but I'm a bit scared that she's going to make me look like a hooker or a drag queen.

Getting ready together turns into a real giggle and reminds me of mine and Denise's time at university. We shared halls in our first year and then lived together for the remaining years. Denise's degree in primary education had her in uni or out at work experience all of the time and she found it funny in our last year when I only had a couple of hour lessons and some one-to-ones with my tutor.

It's weird to think that she's now working in her profession and has been for a number of years while I'm still treading water at Holborns. Thinking about all of this begins to bring me down.

Suddenly a sock hits me in the face pulling me back to reality. I glare at Sara but remember Lewis's face and burst into laughter. The drinks continue to flow freely and I find myself more inebriated than I had anticipated by the time everyone is ready. We all look great, although a bit overdressed for a mere strategizing meal.

The Travel Lodge is really central and so there are loads of restaurants, pubs and shops nearby.

'Let's go to that Harvester we saw as we came in,' Jenna instructs. I feel my irritation bubble up as she takes control again.

'Yeah okay, sounds good,' Denise agrees, because she's always so accommodating, even if she didn't want to go there, she would still agree. I wish she would speak up for herself a bit more sometimes. Although her kind heart is what endeared her to me in the first place.

As soon as we enter The Harvester it's abundantly clear we are way too dressed up to be in here, especially on a Monday night. The locals glare and leer at us as we walk across the room to find a table and I get the impression we're not very welcome.

'Alright love, have you been to a wedding?' A charming man at the bar asks me, snickering under his breath. And just like that I feel silly. He's right, why have we got ourselves so dressed up just to have dinner? It must be all the drink we had while getting ready. My cheeks flare and I think how their redness must be clashing with the blue eye shadow Sara insisted went with this outfit. I find myself instinctively rubbing at my face, trying to dull down the make-up and I feel embarrassed walking back to our table.

'Right what's our plan of action?' Sara taps her fingers on the table, commanding all attention on her. We've huddled into a corner booth that was the only free table; the pub is strangely busy for a Monday evening.

'Let's get some food first,' I say trying to delay the inevitable, I make a show of scouring the menu and everyone turns their attention to their menus. Finally, I choose a chicken burger and chips. I hope the bun will soak up some of the alcohol because the wine has really gone to my head.

'Right then, what is our plan?' Jenna starts, once we've placed our order then turns towards me to see what I want to do.

'Like I said before I'm not sure this is a good idea,' I try to backtrack. What am I doing here? Sara's powers of persuasion are too good.

'Oh not that crap again,' Sara sighs, holding up her hand in exasperation.

'We're here now, Alma, we might as well go and do it. Or at least find him?' Denise adds softly.

'Too bloody right I didn't drive all this way for nothing. Alma, you're doing it. It'll be good for you,' Jenna states.

'Okay, okay.' I don't think I have any choice. I feel like this trip is getting out of hand. How did we end up here? I didn't think this was a good idea in the first place.

'Well, I thought we'd go to his parents' house about 8am,' Sara suggests. 'That way if he does live there, which he might, we can catch him before work. You'll have to look amazing of course, Alma. So I think we'll need to get up at 6am.' Sara outlines her plans while everyone looks on in wonder, she really has thought this through. I hadn't got much further than the drive.

'6am?' Jenna gasps. I bet she was hoping for a lie in. I smirk to myself. The one time she doesn't have to do the school run and she still has to get up early.

'Yeah, why don't we go a bit later? And what's going to take two hours? We're only a fifteen-minute drive away, surely 7am would be enough?' With any luck Nick won't be there and I can avoid the whole messy thing. He probably doesn't live there anyway. I hope.

'Fine we can get up at 6.30am, but no later. Come on girls, we're here on a mission and we can go back to bed once we've done it. Let's go early and catch him. It's probably our best bet,' she explains. 'In the evening he could be out.'

Reluctantly we all agree to Sara's crazy plan, it does actually make some sense. I can feel the bile rise up in my stomach at the thought of seeing Nick again. I know we all talked about this happening but it's all happening very fast and feeling very real now and it's freaking me out. I'd better make sure I look absolutely stunning.

My thoughts are interrupted by our food coming and I hope that I can eat something because I suddenly don't feel very hungry. We all tuck in and the conversation comes to a halt. As I begin to eat, my stomach changes its mind and I begin to feel a lot better. About halfway through the meal I finally realise why the pub is so packed. The screens are all turned on and the football commentary starts belting in our ears. It's so loud I can't hear anything other than the football. We decide to find somewhere else to chat once we've finished. Apparently, we're not ready to call it a night yet.

We search up and down the streets and end up in a trendy bar called Soho. I regard Sara suspiciously, I bet this was her plan all along, especially with the clothes and how dressed up we all are. A few more cocktails and spirits in us and there goes my plan not to mix my drinks and we end up in the local club. It must be after midnight now, so much for a quiet night. We all crowd onto the dance floor, pop our handbags in the middle and have a good dance. The floor is sticky under foot and I'm once again reminded of my uni days, although this time my heels are definitely staying on and I won't be out till 4am.

The club is quite busy for a Monday. Apparently, the football ended in our favour meaning everyone is in a celebratory mood and it gives the club a really good vibe. As we dance, I can see men surrounding us and as I look over at Sara she turns and starts snogging the face off a random man. He looks a bit like the hulk but younger and with a handlebar moustache and huge muscles, although obviously he's not green. His friend comes over to me as Denise and Jenna excuse themselves to go to the loos.

'Hey, I'm Eric, what's your name?' He gives me a cheeky grin and tries to get closer. I can tell he's trying to dance with me but he's really not my type even though I've had too much to drink, I still know what I like. I wish I'd gone to the toilets with the girls now.

'Hi, I'm Alma,' I say trying to subtly move myself away without offending him but also making it clear I'm not interested in him in that way.

'You girls come here often.' Eric laughs at his own cheesy pick-up line and I have to concentrate not to roll my eyes.

'No, we're not from round here,' I say bluntly, trying not to continue the conversation further.

'What are you doing here then?' he asks, his tone has changed and I can tell he's irritated that I'm not fawning all over him. I try to catch Sara's eye but her face is still suctioned onto Hulk's. Great. Where are Jenna and Denise, it feels like they've been gone forever.

I don't want to tell him we're here to see my ex and find out why he ghosted me. 'Just for a girls' weekend, thought it would be fun.' I smile, hoping that will be the end of it.

'It's Monday,' he says deadpan and I can tell he's completely lost interest in me. He's looking around now for his next victim and I move a little further away. A little blonde girl spins around and I see him swoon and I know he'll be off soon.

'I'm going to get a drink anyway,' he says and I watch him approach the little blonde, well *he's* obviously a catch.

I hover next to Sara and Hulk as they moon over each other and I feel increasingly uncomfortable, awkward and suddenly sober. At least when I was talking to Eric I wasn't completely alone.

After another fifteen minutes I see Jenna and Denise wandering back over, I'm irritated they've been gone for so long.

'Where the hell have you two been?' I snap, not able to hide my annoyance.

'Oh sorry,' Denise says sheepishly. 'We got a bit lost and the queue to the toilets was huge. It's so loud and busy in here,' Denise adds, looking around. I know this isn't really her scene anymore. She's been settled down with Jay for five years and their favourite thing to do is chill out, order in and watch Netflix. I wish I had someone to do that with.

I shrug it off because there's no point in letting it ruin our evening, they're here now and we can all enjoy ourselves. I'm ready to have a bit more of a dance and I start to move around. I look over at Jenna who looks a bit pinched, this probably isn't her scene either come to think of it. I bet she's been complaining to Denise about it. She does look quite flushed.

'I think I'm going to head back,' Jenna cuts into my train of thought.

'Oh okay.' I'm quite relieved she is going. If Denise stays, I could have a good dance with her and then head back to bed.

'I'll come too,' says Denise. 'I don't want you going back on your own.'

'Oh, I guess I'll come too then,' I say, not wanting to be left alone with Sara and Hulk again. 'Let's see if Sara's coming to the hotel with us or back to his.'

As it turns out, we all head back to the hotel, Sara included as apparently Hulk wasn't *that* good a kisser. Could have had me fooled, she certainly checked thoroughly to be sure.

We slump into bed and my mind turns to Nick. I think about the last time I saw him and how we kissed and said goodbye. The last time I saw him we were in love, at least I thought we were. Now a year later I'm finally going to see him again. This feels surreal. What am I doing?

Chapter 10

I wake up the next morning and I feel vile. A loud bleeping noise is coming from the lump that is Sara. I glance in the mirror across the room; my face looks like a drag queen has been hauled through a bush and my hair doesn't look much better. My head is absolutely pounding, I can hear my heart in my ears with every beat. I sniff the air and I can definitely smell sick. I cautiously run my tongue over my teeth to confirm it. Yes, I was sick last night. But where?

'Why is that going off so early?' Sara croaks. She chose this time. Cheeky bitch.

'Because you set it to make us get up so we can catch him before work,' I whinge, still trying to work out where the sick smell is coming from. Maybe I made it to the loo but didn't flush. I hope so.

It's been a long time since I've been this hung over, I must've been quite drunk. I reach down and grab my handbag before taking a tentative look inside in case that's where the sick smell is coming from. Why can't I remember?

'Did I? No. Oh, yeah, I remember,' Sara backtracks.

'Right let's get to it then, we need to make you look amazing.' I turn over and that's when I realise, Jenna is turned on her side facing away from me and the back of her pyjama top is covered in sick. She moves and the smell is released further. What do I do? I debate trying to pass it off as her sick but I know she won't buy that.

'Jenna, you might want to hop in the shower.' As I speak, she turns over and rolls in sick. I put my hand over my mouth, she's going to be so mad. I see her put her hand down and realisation dawns. She jumps out of bed and looks at me furiously. 'Was that you? That's disgusting you've thrown up on me,' she shouts and runs into the bathroom. This would never have happened if I'd had my own bed, or room for that matter, I think bitterly.

The others look at me and I shrug on my way to the phone to call the front desk. I'm going to have to do some serious grovelling; I hope they'll change the sheets whilst we're gone.

An hour later and I don't look so rough. Jenna is still pretty mad and I can totally understand why although I have apologised profusely. I could have definitely done with another five hours of sleep but this will have to do. I'm dressed in jeans and a top at my own insistence aware that wearing a party dress at 8am on someone's doorstep is just weird. Even if it looks good, thank you Sara.

After a bit of circling around we find Nick's parents' house. My stomach is doing flip flops and I'm certain now that this is the craziest and worst idea anyone has ever had. We park a bit down the street from his house so I'll have to walk the last few metres. I feel like I'm going to hyperventilate because the nerves are really getting to me now. What *am* I doing?

'I don't think I can do this.' I say, trying to steady my breathing. I look pleadingly at the girls. 'Please don't make me do this.'

'I knew you'd need another pep talk.' Sara smiles, she's clearly ready for this. 'What have you got to lose? You're not happy, are you?'

Before I can answer Jenna butts in, 'Since Nick broke your heart you haven't been happy, have you? You have a miserable career you dread in admin; you barely take any photographs and that's what you really used to love, you live at home with Mum and Dad and the only date you've been on since was Lewis the Loo Loser.' And like that Jenna sums up my miserable life. I can feel the tears start to sting my eyes. This trip was supposed to be fun. I didn't realise all of my life choices were going to be under such scrutiny. It appears it's not just my love life I'm getting wrong but my career, clothes and living situation too.

'She's right, Alma, I'm sorry. You're coasting along, you've lost your passion. He took that from you. Go and get it back. Get your power back. You look amazing, show him what he's missing. Get your answers and the closure you need to properly move on.' The determination in Denise's eyes surprises me. I didn't realise this was what people thought of me, this is what my sad little life looks like to my friends.

They think I'm a right loser. They're right I have lost my power, my passion. I was such a different girl when I met Nick and the way he left me broke my heart and destroyed my confidence. A different feeling comes over me and I realise it's not just sadness but anger.

How dare he get away with it all. He just left and ignored me. He never told me why. He never had to tell me it was over; the gutless weasel just left and never bothered with me again. Didn't even send me a text to say we were finished. Imagine how uncomfortable he will be when he sees me and realises I want answers and he finally has to face up to what he did. I won't let him belittle me; I deserve more than this. The girls are right.

'Also, if you don't go knock on that door I will. And Alma, I cannot be held responsible for what comes out of my mouth,' Sara adds, to seal the deal.

That's it, I need to go in. I don't want Sara fighting my battles and anyway she's too unpredictable. I need to hear the excuses straight from the horse's mouth.

I walk up to Nick's parents' front door. I feel sick. I knock tentatively on the door. No one answers. After all of that, no one answers. Well that's that then. I walk back over to the car.

'Right, you're going back and knocking properly,' Sara starts, clearly not impressed with me.

'What? I did,' I whine, hovering outside the car by Sara's open window.

'You did not. There's no way they heard that. Stroking the door and coming back here does not count as trying. Go back now and knock properly.' Sara waves wildly at the house gesturing for me to do as she says.

Jenna locks the car doors. 'She's right we're not letting you back in this car until you do it right.'

I groan, trust Jenna to join in.

'I have to agree, Alma. Just go knock again and if they're not in then they're not in,' Denise says.

I slowly walk back over to the house, my head down like a child that's had a good telling off. I give it a good loud knock; I don't want there to be any confusion this time. I wait. I'm just about ready to give up when I hear some shuffling and swearing from behind the door whilst someone tries to find the key and fumbles to put it in the lock. There's a big lump in my throat. What if it's Nick?

But it's not Nick, it's his Mum, Jane, who answers the door. There's no mistaking she is his mother, they have the same piercing blue eyes and long noses. She's wearing a dressing gown and I can see my knocking has roused her from a deep sleep.

This isn't the way I had imagined us meeting. This isn't how I thought this would happen. We had plans to go and meet both sets of parents before we settled down. He was to come to Twinton for a week after meeting me off the ship that last day, and then I was to come up and meet his family in Linkley. I briefly wonder if we would have gotten on, under better circumstances, where I'm not a stranger on the doorstep.

'Yes?' she says gruffly. Her hair is sticking up in funny places and there are indents on her face from her pillow. 'Look whatever you're selling I'm not buying.'

I just stand there staring and I see her go to close the door. Instinctively I stick my foot out. I've come here for answers and I need to get them. She looks down at my foot and frowns, the expression on her face hardening.

'I.. I.. I'm looking for Nick?' I finally stammer.

'Okay, well he doesn't live here.' She goes to close the door again but my foot isn't budging.

'You are his mum though? Jane?' I ask, searching her face but I know she is.

'Yes. Look if you're a friend of his why don't you just give him a call or something.' She's woken up a bit more now and I can see her appraising me. Here goes nothing; I'm going to tell her who I am. She must have heard of me when we were together, we had plans.

'I'm Alma. Do you have a number or address I can reach him on?' I ask. I wait for the realisation, the recognition of my name, of who I am to register on her face but it doesn't come.

'I've never heard of an Alma, wait there.' She turns back into the house. I can hear her mumbling in the background 'Donald... Donald.... Have you heard of an Alma? Knows Nick *apparently*.' She casts her eyes back over me.

Donald comes to the door standing next to his wife. 'Look love, neither of us has ever heard of you,' he says softly. 'We're not giving out his details willy nilly. If you've got a message for him you can write it on this piece of paper and we'll ask him to get back to you. He's coming over in the next few days.'

'Oh, well I was rather hoping to speak to him in person,' I say. 'Could you not just give me his number? I really need to speak with him,' I plead, sounding pathetic.

'Right, well I'm really not comfortable with all of this. If you're his friend you should already have his number, surely? To be honest you've woken us up at God knows what hour and I think you'd better leave now,' he says, turning stern. I take my foot out of the door because I don't want to cause a scene, no doubt the neighbours' curtains are twitching.

I head back to the car with my head down. That did not go well. After psyching myself up for a showdown with Nick I'm utterly deflated.

I get back into the car with the girls and we drive around the corner to the local greasy spoon for a fry up and to discuss our next move. It's in walking distance of Nick's parents' house but I doubt this is the kind of place they frequent and certainly not at this hour. I give my friends a blow by blow account of the conversation.

'Well that's it, isn't it?' Denise's eyes light up.

I look blankly between Sara and Jenna not understanding what Denise is thinking. They both shrug, seemingly unaware too.

'Stakeout,' she says. 'They said he's coming over in the next few days. We wait outside his parents' house, loads of snacks and so on and we can catch him when he comes to see them.' Denise and her crime programmes, she has really gone mad this time. I look at Jenna and Sara and they're nodding along.

'Great idea,' says Jenna.

'It's brilliant,' agrees Sara. 'That way he will still be on the back foot and not expecting to see you.'

'That's assuming that his parents haven't called him about a crazy girl called Alma who they know nothing about.' I still can't believe they have never heard of me. He told me he'd emailed them and talked on the phone about me. What a lying piece of shit.

I can't see the point in arguing about the stakeout.

'Fine, let's do a stakeout,' I say, resigned to my fate and even more furious with Nick.

After we've filled ourselves up on a grease and carbs breakfast, we head out to the local shops and stock up on snacks and drinks. We park a bit up the road so they can't see us. Time passes slowly and not much seems to happen and we could be doing this for days. There's no one going into or out of his house. We see his Dad go out to take the bins in at one point and we all quickly duck down inside the car. Everyone erupts into giggles, now it feels like a proper stakeout. We're all wearing sunglasses even though it's not sunny.

Every so often a few of us pop off to the local pub for a wee and a little drink. We started off with soft drinks but as the day has gone on and through boredom we've turned to alcohol. Slowly over the day we have all become more and more intoxicated, except Jenna, who's driving. Looking in the mirror now on one of my many trips to the loos, I can see that my make-up has begun to melt due to spending so much time in the warm car. The main thing that is helping me through all of this is the alcohol.

Hair of the dog indeed.

Finally, at 6pm we see him go into the house. It's Denise who spots him first and the atmosphere in the car is close to hysteria. It's the moment of truth now. After all this time and heartache, I'm going to get my answers. Sara gets out of the car and opens my door, ready to manhandle me out if I don't get out myself but she needn't bother. I'm ready. I step out of the car and walk up to the house; the drinks have boosted my courage. I knock on the door. Donald answers.

'Oh hello, you again,' he says deadpan and looking puzzled. 'Nick,' he shouts.

Nick arrives at the door. As soon as he sees me his mouth drops open and I can see he's in a state of shock. I'm probably the last person he expected to see. I smile, enjoying catching him unawares.

'Dad, you can go back in, I'll be there in a minute,' Nick says, shooing his Dad away from the door. Perhaps he doesn't want him to hear this, to know what kind of a man he is, what kind of a man he has raised.

I clear my throat. I'm ready to ask my questions. I'm ready to find out what happened, why he ghosted me. Ask him how he could have been so cruel but he cuts me short.

'Look, I don't know why you're here but you have to go. I'm not interested in talking to you.' He slams the door in my face and locks it. I'm so shocked that I stand there like a fish, my mouth involuntarily opening and closing. What now? Tears sting my eyes; we came here for this? Is that it? Where's my closure? Fuck it. I knock again. My knocking is quiet with uncertainty at first and then it erupts into loud bangs. I'm practically beating the shit out of the door now. I'm shouting and out of breath from all the exertions after being so sedentary all day. I look up to see his Mum hanging out of the bedroom window shouting at me. I stop banging and look up trying to fathom what she's saying, my drunk mind swimming. I must look a right state and I'm putting on a real show for the neighbours now.

'IF YOU DON'T LEAVE NOW, I AM GOING TO CALL THE POLICE. STALKING IS ILLEGAL, YOU KNOW.'

I look up ready to defend myself, ready to say something. What did she say? Stalking? I'm not a stalker. But instead Jane empties a bucket of water over me. I see her reach back for another bucket and I run back to the car. Now I'm soaked and I still don't have my closure. Nick has made his parents think I'm some kind of stalker, painted himself as a good man. A victim.

Fucking liar.

Chapter 11

I slump back in the car. Wet and defeated. I knew this was a bad idea. I can't believe I let them talk me into it. Look at me now, I'm like a drowned rat and all for nothing.

'Oh, Alma,' Denise coos, watching the silent tears stream down my face.

It's over. I'm never going to know why he did it. I'll never get my closure. He's getting away with it all over again. He doesn't care, the way looked at me was like a slap in the face. I'm mortified.

'We could just wait here? Wait until he comes out to go home? We could...' Sara suggests, trailing off in a quiet voice as I stare her down until she stops speaking.

It's too late, I'm soaked and he wouldn't speak to me anyway. Even worse his parents might call the police. Imagine that, he'd probably convince *them* I'm a stalker too and they'll take me in for questioning.

'No. Let's go back to the hotel. I just want to crawl into bed and die,' I say, knowing I'm being melodramatic but not caring anyway.

The girls don't dare say a word. I wish that I was

going to my own bed in my own room. I want to be at home in my own little space away from the world. Away from everyone. I imagine myself back home curled up in my huge quilt, snug and safe. I can't help but also imagine Mum hovering outside, pressing her ear to the door. No place is my own.

The atmosphere in the car is tense. I'm so low I don't want to speak. I huddle in the corner trying to get warm but staying cold to the core. We all sit in silence for the short drive back. Defeated.

Once back at the hotel I put my hand out to Jenna for the key fob, snatch it from her fingers and walk quickly to the room. I don't look back at the girls, I keep my head down and I can hear them all panting and struggling to keep up with my fast pace.

In the safety of our shared room I have a shower, letting the water wash away my tears. I stand in the shower until the water turns cold and I hear a light tap on the door and a mumbling about the toilet. I don't rush. I've got nowhere to be and despite knowing they had the best of intentions I can't help but blame my friends. My life was fine before all of this happened. Maybe a bit bland to an outsider, but I was happy. Well, maybe not happy, but content. Yes, I was content. Now I don't know what to do with myself. Now it's all too clear that my life is a big mess. That I am failing.

I'm even more humiliated than before. Not quietly, like when Nick ghosted me. Everyone wondering and whispering behind my back, not a word to my face. No, this time it's been an elaborate stage show for everyone to see. I should really take a bow. This is so much worse. I think about Nick slamming the door in my face and I cringe at his Mum pouring water over me. What did I think he was going to do? Get down on his knees and apologise for being a prick? Tell me he regrets it every day? That maybe he still loves me? I probe deeper, exploring my feelings for the first time in a long time. Is that what I wanted from him? For him to still love me, because I still love him? Or do I hate him?

This whole trip has really made me question things I had so carefully pushed down and hidden away. I was better off before. I'd come to terms with it, accepted it even.

I finally step out of the shower and wrap myself in the big, fluffy, hotel towel. As I walk back into the room Sara darts for the loo. I know she's treating this seriously because instead of banging the door down to get in she waited and only tapped lightly. It's not like Sara to be so restrained. I would laugh if I wasn't so desperate to cry.

I walk over to my bed, thank God room service has changed the sheets and it's not covered in sick anymore. I'm sure I'll be charged for that. Great. Another good thing about this trip to add to the list.

Denise and Jenna watch me tentatively, I see their mouths open and close as I pull the covers up and over my head trying my hardest to hide away. I hope they get the hint and leave me alone.

Sara comes barrelling back into the room. 'Come on mate, let's go and have a drink or something. We at least need dinner?' she suggests, trying to cajole me into getting up, but it's no good I'm not moving for the night.

'No appetite,' I say bluntly. I turn away under the

covers. 'You go though. I'd like to be alone.'

'Are you sure?' Jenna asks, placing a hand on my back. I don't want her to touch me. I don't even know why she's here. I don't want to talk to *her* about it. *They* made me come and where am I? Worse off than before. I've allowed Nick to make a fool out of me. Again.

'Do you want me to stay?' Denise asks in a soft voice. 'Do you want to talk about it?'

'No. No, you all go. I mean it.' I try to keep my voice light so they can all leave and I can succumb to the tears that are brimming. They reluctantly leave the room telling me to call if I need anything and reassure me that they're here if I need to talk.

I don't want to talk, talking got me the horrible date with Lewis the Loo Loser and another heart thrashing from Nick the Prick. I don't need to talk right now. I think about how sad everything has become; this was supposed to be about getting my power back but Nick has singlehandedly taken it away completely. How could I have loved someone so heartless, so indifferent, who won't even give me an explanation?

I'm dumbfounded that his parents never knew about me. Was every little thing he ever told me a lie? How will I ever be able to trust anyone ever again? I feel the deceit and hurt so sharply now it's like a physical pain. I lie still on my side and wait for sleep, trying desperately to empty my mind but it keeps going back to him trying to pass me off to his parents as a psycho stalker.

I replay our relationship over in my mind just as I have so many times before, trying to see if there were any signs that I missed. Was he really that into me, or did I imagine the whole thing? I'm so confused. Nick chased me for weeks before I agreed to go on a date with him. *He* chased *me*. Even though I was attracted to him straight away I could see lots of the girls fancied him and I didn't want to be messed around. I imagined him to be a player. He had the looks and confidence but he was always true to me. After all, everyone knows everything about each other on a ship.

You live together, work together and play together. There's really nowhere to hide. He pursued me; he was the one who said I love you first, him, not me. My heart hurts as I remember him saying those words to me. The image of him standing in his cabin after a night at the crew bar is so vivid. I laughed it off at first, believing that he was just drunk but he said it again in the morning and I found myself saying it back. We had such a good connection and from that moment on if we weren't working, we were barely apart. In the ports of call, in the crew bar or going out for dinner on the rare occasions I had the night off. He'd often come and visit me when I was working in the photo gallery or on a photoshoot. I trusted him completely.

What a fool.

I sob myself to sleep.

I wake the next morning with a growling stomach, puffy eyes and another sore head but this one is from all the crying. I heard the girls come back late at night so I would guess they won't be ready to leave right away. I sigh, I just want to get back home. I roll over and see Jenna sleeping soundly, her blonde hair spread all over the pillow, not a worry in the world. Sara is snoring and Denise is also flat out. I get up and go and splash some water on my puffy eyes. My movement rouses Jenna.

'You alright?' she croaks; someone has definitely been drinking. Here I am with my heart breaking and she's been out on the lash, charming. Some sister. A wave of bitterness engulfs me and it takes all my effort not to bite her head off. I don't know why she's even here on this trip.

'Yeah, yeah fine. When do you think we could head off?' I ask, choking down my anger and gritting my teeth. If I can just get home, I should be able to avoid her for a while. I'm going to need to keep her sweet though so she won't tell Mum what's happened. I flinch at the thought of Mum trying to discuss this all with me. That's just what I need. Not.

'Oh um, probably not till late afternoon, I had a few too many last night and I don't think it'd be safe for me to drive,' she says, looking embarrassed.

I can feel my cheeks burn with anger. Great, let's prolong the agony. Why did they go out drinking? I know I said I wanted to be left alone but I think that's really insensitive.

'Oh. Okay,' I murmur. I keep my voice flat to hide my real thoughts.

She looks up but doesn't say anything. Our talking has woken Sara and Denise who don't look quite as bad as Jenna. Perhaps they weren't all drinking. Just my darling sister.

'Hey. I know you're feeling down but why don't we turn the trip around and go for a shop?' Sara asks. 'We've got some time to kill anyway.'

'Yeah, that's a good idea. I've looked and they have a shopping outlet here which is supposed to be really good, full of designer bargains,' Denise adds, trying to sense my mood and keep her tone light. 'We could check out, pop our bags in the car and head out?'

'Yes okay,' I say. What have I got to lose? Maybe a bit of retail therapy will make me feel better, it certainly couldn't make me feel worse. If we're stuck here anyway, I'd rather be shopping than talking.

We get dressed, only this time no one comments on my horrible, hair, dress or make-up. I purposefully dress in my drabbest clothes, the grey baggy jumper and jogging bottoms I brought to slob in our hotel room, daring them to say something. No one does.

The brisk twenty-minute walk to the outlet wakes us all up. I can feel everyone treading on eggshells around me and see concern written all over the faces. I've now gone past the point of blaming them for this trip so I try to lift myself up a bit for their sakes as well as my own. No need for this to be a *totally* miserable trip.

We go to a fast food place in the outlet and sit down with a feast. I suddenly feel ravenous and am looking forward to stuffing my face. The conversation is light at first, talking about everything but the elephant in the room. I mostly stay quiet and only talk when really needed. After we've finished our meal and are all out of small talk Jenna turns to me.

'Never mind, Alma, it could be worse. I never thought this was a good idea anyway,' she says.

Is that supposed to be her thinly veiled attempt at comfort? What the hell? She wasn't even invited on this trip anyway and she never said this wasn't a good idea. I don't even know why she came. She's not even my friend. I can feel the anger bubbling beneath the surface and rising into my chest. It bursts out of me before I have a chance to stop it and I'm stunned that I yell it at her.

'WHY DID YOU FUCKING COME THEN? I NEVER FUCKING INVITED YOU ANYWAY. NO

ONE WANTS YOU HERE.'

How fucking dare she belittle my experience, my life, my feelings. She has no idea what I'm going through. Her with her perfect life. Her perfect husband. Perfect kids. What the fuck does she know about pain? I wait for her response, wait for her to shout at me like she did when she was a teenager, but she doesn't. She looks like a deer caught in the headlights. Stunned. I can see the cogs turning in her mind and her expression changes. Tears begin to fill her eyes. I'm shocked, it's not like her to cry. Oh great, now I look like a monster in front of Sara and Denise. Thanks Jenna.

She's probably trying for the sympathy vote because I shouted at her in front of them. Surely she can't be this upset. She must know she wasn't really invited. Without a word she scrapes her chair back but it catches on something and falls to the floor, making a loud clanging noise. She looks at it debating whether to pick it up. All of the diners around us are staring, the few that weren't looking after I shouted are now straining their necks with curiosity after the clanging chair. I put my head in my hands and tentatively look between my fingers at Denise and Sara whose mouths are popping open and shut, looking from me to Jenna in shock. Jenna starts to run away.

Denise and Sara quickly compose themselves and Denise gets up, running swiftly after Jenna. I feel my rage return at Jenna monopolising my friends yet again.

'I'm all about telling your truth, but that was harsh,' Sara says staring me down. 'We never said we didn't want her here. You don't speak for me.'

I look down at my hands, they're red raw where I've involuntarily been scratching them as this whole thing has unfolded. Sara has snapped me back to reality and

I can't quite believe what I've just done. I don't want to hear this; I don't want to know. I don't want Sara to tell me how it is.

I get up and leave, walking in the opposite direction to Jenna, not daring to look back.

Chapter 12

I wander aimlessly around the outlet. Now what? Now what do I do? Great, so I've fallen out with my friends and my sister in one fell swoop. I go down the escalator to the lower level and sit at the fountain in the centre of the outlet. I watch the people go about their business, the hustle and bustle. I used to love people watching but as life has moved on, I've not tended to do it so much. I sit here for what must be hours, although I don't look at a clock. I finally pull out my phone to check but the battery's dead.

I've no interest in looking for Jenna, Sara and Denise, I just can't face them. I can't believe my friends have taken Jenna's side. Have they not heard her endless swipes at me? Judging me from her high *perfect* horse.

I brush the thoughts aside and try to concentrate instead on the people walking past. I make up stories in my mind about what the people are doing and where they're going. I see a young couple walking hand in hand, so sweet, I decide they're first loves and at that stage where life hasn't yet made them cynical, and everything is wonderful, romantic and intense. *He* isn't a pathological liar and everything is perfect. I see an older man hurrying past in a suit, he's on his way to the office to work for his powerful female boss, oh yes. I see a woman and a toddler; she's holding his little pudgy hand and he's dragging his little feet along the floor. I bet he's had enough of shopping and wants to go home and is only moments away from a full-on tantrum.

Then another woman catches my eye, she's hurrying past laden with bags on both arms. Slim and graceful with long blonde hair scraped up in a messy bun. I really start to scrutinise her; she looks just like Kelly. It's uncanny. But it can't be. Why would she be here? As she walks past I see the back of her and that's when I spot it, a little heart tattoo on the back of her neck. That woman doesn't just look like Kelly. She *is* Kelly. I know because I have the same heart tattoo on the back of my neck. We got them when we were on the world cruise together, we'd become so close at that point and we thought it would be a fun thing to do in port one day.

I start to follow Kelly, hurrying along to catch up with her. Whilst I'd been staring opened mouthed, she's managed to walk quite far away and I have to jog to catch up. Now I really am some kind of stalker. I'm so confused. The last I heard from Kelly was that she was on a ship in Australia. Well I may have fallen out with my other friends today but now I've found Kelly. Maybe she's meant to be here to cheer me up, like a fairy Godmother sent just when I need a friend the most. I feel a bit brighter already.

As I get closer, I call, 'Kelly, Kelly,' as loud as I can and a few people turn to look at all the noise I'm making. I must look a right state in my drab clothes but I don't care. Kelly's seen me at my worst. I think back to that horrible day at the terminal when *he* didn't turn up.

She looks around trying to find the source of her name and eventually her eyes lock with mine. I can see she's surprised to see me; her mouth hangs open for a moment and she looks around uncomfortably. She shakes it off and recovers, it must be as much of a shock for her to see me as it is for me to see her.

'Oh, er hello,' Kelly says brightly and, dropping her bags to the floor, leans in to give me a hug. It's lovely to see her. 'Um, what are you doing up here? This is crazy,' she says, looking around again.

'Oh, just a visit. Bit of shopping and whatnot,' I say, not wanting to go into the whole sorry mess. She knew Nick and me as a couple and witnessed first-hand the humiliation of Nick standing me up. I'm not ready to go into it all standing in the middle of a shopping outlet.

'Well, it's been nice to see you. I've really got to head off. I'm late for an appointment,' she says bending down to pick up her bags.

'Oh, I see. Do you live here?' I ask, puzzled. I thought she lived in Manchester. 'I could walk with you if you like?' I continue, not wanting her to leave just yet. It's nice to have someone to talk to. A friendly face. What are the chances that she would be here? 'We could arrange to meet up later, go for a chat? After your appointment?' I suggest, not letting her get a word in. I must look desperate. I finally look to her for an answer. If she can meet me later I'll just catch the train back alone, the girls aren't exactly my biggest fans at the moment, they'll probably be pleased.

'Oh, um yes that sounds good. My number's the same. I better go. We can have a proper chat later.' She begins to hurry away turning her head to and fro. She looks almost manic. In her hurry she's dropped one of her bags. I pick it up and go after her.

'Wait, your bag.' I jog to catch up.

Kelly spins around to retrieve it and suddenly her expression hardens and her eyes dilate. The change is so subtle that if I hadn't been staring so intently at her face, I could have missed it. Kelly first looks at me, then over my shoulder. Shaking her head her eyes fill with water and she looks back at me. 'I'm so sorry, you were never meant to find out this way. Or at all really.'

I look at her, confused. What is she talking about? I turn to see what she's looking at. That's when I see him.

Nick.

Striding over, without a care in the world, all smug and confident. A baby strapped to his front and a smoothie in both hands. He hasn't noticed me yet. I look quite a state, still puffy eyed from last night. All baggy clothes and messy hair, not stylishly messy either, like Kelly's. He probably doesn't even recognise me. I consider walking away, but curiosity has got the better of me. I can't quite work it out.

'What the fuck is going on?' I ask Kelly, looking between Kelly and Nick and the baby. The baby? Nick's baby?

As Nick arrives, he looks straight at Kelly, not even registering my existence. Dismissing me like I'm some poor beggar woman, not good enough to even be noticed.

'All right love, I think Griff is getting hungry,' he says, looking down. 'Do you want Mummy to take you?' He coos over the baby. Then turns and notices me for the first time.

Mummy? I take a good look at the baby now. Kelly could well be Mummy but there's no mistaking who Daddy is. He has the same shaped nose and eyes; the baby is Nick's double. Mouthing happily, content on his chest. I don't know much about babies, I think back to when Claire and Sam were newborns barely able to support their own heads, so small. This baby does not look like a newborn. My head starts to swim and I mentally begin to do the maths. It's been a year since we left the ship, nine months to carry a baby and this baby certainly looks over three months. Oh my God; they were having an affair?

All the colour has drained from Kelly's face and she's standing there speechless, mouth dropping. Not even answering Nick.

Nick finally registers who I am, his mouth dropping open too. And it all starts to fall into place. This is why he stopped talking to me.

Nick and Kelly. Kelly and Nick.

I start to mull it all over in my mind but I'm gobsmacked. What the fuck? Nick's face is a picture. He probably thought he'd already dealt with me, dispensed with me yesterday, yet here I am again.

Now I'm going to get some answers.

'How long was this going on for?' I ask him. 'How could you?' I say to Kelly. I feel like I've been physically winded, all the air has gone out of me and I'm not sure whether I need to sit down or throw up. But I hold my own, waiting to hear an explanation. Waiting for my closure. I may have fucked everything up but I'm getting my closure now.

Kelly looks down, she won't meet my gaze. I still

can't believe it. I must be wrong. I stand there turning my head from one to the other, waiting. I'm fuming. I feel as though steam might be coming out of my ears.

'So this is why you stopped talking to me. You gutless piece of shit. Why wouldn't you just tell me?' I'm still trying to piece it all together and get my head around it. When? When did they have time for this? And a baby?

Nick shrugs. 'We were only together eight months. It's not a big deal. Get over it,' he adds coldly, dismissing me like I was nothing to him. I know that wasn't the case.

'No. Nick, no. I will not let you pretend it all meant nothing to you, we were in love. *You* were going to meet my family. I was going to move here. Don't you dare pretend it was nothing,' I snap and then turn to Kelly. 'And as for you, what the fuck? Had a good laugh at me, did you? You pretended you were in Australia and all the time you were really here having Nick's baby? You utter bitch.' My heart is beating wildly in my chest but it feels good to get it all out. I think I'm more heartbroken over Kelly. I thought she was my friend and I can't believe she did this to me.

Griff has sensed the atmosphere and starts to cry. Kelly and Nick awkwardly navigate the drinks and the baby and Griff is settled in Kelly's arms while I stand waiting and watching. I can't believe they have a baby together. I'm looking at what I thought would be my future with Nick and I can't believe it. Did they really hate me so much that they wouldn't just tell me?

'I never thought you would find out, to be honest,' Kelly starts, gently rocking Griff in her arms, trying to keep her voice quiet. 'I didn't know Nick was *that* much of a big deal to you. I thought you'd moved on. You never mentioned him in your emails. And I didn't lie, I did have a contract to go to Australia I just never went and you assumed. So…' She trails off letting the betrayal hang in the air.

'So, what is this?' I ask gesturing between them. 'Were you two having an affair behind my back the whole time?' I can't seem to make sense of it, my head hurts the more I think about it. I don't know whether to laugh or cry.

'It only happened once,' Kelly starts. 'We didn't want to hurt you.'

'BULLSHIT,' I shout, it's so loud a few shoppers stop and stare but I can't help myself. 'Why wouldn't you just tell me? You came and sat with me at the terminal. That was fucking cruel. How did you not hurt me?' I say looking her hard in the eye.

'Well, I loved him too. You never thought about that though, did you?' It's true that when she first came on the ship she'd liked the look of Nick too, but he chose me and she never said anything. She loved him? A lot of the girls had liked the look of him but he chose me.

'Oh, so I deserved what I got, did I? I blamed myself. I thought it was because of something I did. I thought I made you not love me but all along you were sneaking around with Kelly. You robbed me of my chance to hate you and move on. You arsehole. You stole my closure. You stole my confidence and you made me question myself.' I can't believe it and yet it's happened. My best friend and my boyfriend were carrying on behind my back.

Kelly had written to me intermittently and never mentioned a word. How can someone be so callous? What Kelly's done feels even more painful than losing Nick. And more of a betrayal.

'Not everything is about *you*,' Kelly says nastily. 'I never expected to get pregnant. It really did only happen once on the ship and when I found out Nick did the right thing and stood by me.'

'So let me get this right. You knew he wasn't going to turn up at the terminal.' I thought Kelly was being the most supportive friend but she was really witnessing the destruction she helped to cause. Laughing at me behind my back.

'Yes, but I sat with you, didn't I? I was a good friend to you, I made sure I was there for you. That you weren't alone. I could have just left you there. We did you a kindness, it meant everyone wasn't talking about you on the ship. Pitying you. Don't you think it was hard for me to hide? Think about what I was going through. I'd just found out I was pregnant.' She practically shrieks the last bit and I'm dumbfounded.

I'm shocked to my core; she actually thinks she was being a good friend. She sat there with Nick's baby in her belly knowing he wasn't coming to the terminal and watched my humiliation.

'Don't for one second pretend you hid it for my benefit. To protect me. You wanted to protect yourselves and not have everyone talking about *you* on board. You're a cruel bitch.'

I can't believe this, there's something wrong with the pair of them. I turn to look at Nick who's been watching the whole exchange with a self-satisfied look creeping over his face. No doubt he's enjoying being fought over. Even clutching a smoothie in each hand, he still manages to look like a smug, arrogant prick.

I can't think why I ever even liked him.

What a wanker. He doesn't even care about the hurt he put me through. He's no catch, God knows why I cried over him. I fight the urge to punch him and wipe that smug look off his face. I go over and take a smoothie out of his hand and throw it in his face with such speed that it splashes all over him. It feels so good. He's stunned and stands there motionless, blinking through the gloop on his face. I swipe the other smoothie from him and slowly pour it over his head and I savour every last minute. Fucking prick.

'Fucking hell,' he splutters, wiping at the smoothie slush all over his face.

I hope he wasn't thirsty. Now there's a smug look on *my* face.

Finally, I smile. 'You know what, it's fine Kelly. You're more than welcome to my *sloppy* seconds. I hope he makes you happy. He's a deceitful, cheating, lying bastard and I just hope the same doesn't happen to you. Remember, it's hard for a leopard to change his spots.' Kelly dips her head in shame. I bet it's already happened to her.

'Oh, and fuck you both,' I say in a cheery tone. I'm elated as I put my shoulders back and turn and walk away. Griff starts to cry even louder, poor baby having them for parents. I take a deep breath; I can finally breathe properly.

Closure: tick.

Chapter 13

I can feel the adrenaline running through my body. Nick and Kelly. Kelly and Nick. And a baby. I can't believe it. What arseholes. I feel excited and crazy, as though I need to run around or lie down or something. I'm spinning. I need to talk to someone. I need to make sense of what's just happened. I can feel myself physically shaking. Sara was right, it was good to get that closure. Why was I so hung up on someone so callous and selfish and who could do that to me?

For the first time I realise that none of this was my fault. Not *my* doing. I didn't say the wrong thing or come on too strongly. I didn't imagine his feelings for me or make up the things he said to me. He made a poor decision one time with Kelly and now they have a baby together. What a gutless wonder, he couldn't even bring himself to tell me. I'm much better off without him. And her. I can't believe Kelly. I think of Denise and Sara, they would never do anything so cruel. I really misjudged her. I won't make that mistake again.

Finally, I have my answers. I don't need to wonder anymore and I can move on. I feel a mixture of happy and sad. I head back to the hotel; I need to talk to the girls. That's if they'll talk to me. I hope I can make amends. That'll show Jenna she was wrong, I think smugly. This trip was a good idea after all. I wince at the thought of Jenna and picture her running off in tears. Maybe I did go a little too far.

Back at the hotel I hunt the car park for Jenna's car. It's nowhere to be seen. Surely they haven't gone off and left me behind. I can't message them because my phone's dead. I wonder if I could ring one of them from Reception? Not unless I can remember a phone number, and who can do that when we store them in our phone contacts. I pace around the car park again. This trip has really been an emotional roller-coaster and I don't know what to do with myself. I can't believe they have left without me. Maybe they haven't. Maybe Jenna has just moved the car. Maybe they have just gone home. Maybe I deserve that after what I said to Jenna.

My mood dips and I feel as though I might start to cry.

I pull myself together, remembering how good it felt to confront Nick. Get a grip, I tell myself as I head off to Reception, maybe there's a message for me there, or maybe they'll have a charger I can borrow.

I'm in luck, Reception does have a charger I can use, providing I sit in Reception and don't waltz off with it. When the receptionist said this he looked at me very pointedly, as though I could be a thief.

I pull out my phone and pop it on charge and it springs back to life. It pings with countless voicemails and texts. There is one from Denise saying that Jenna is really upset and she's going to head back with her and she hopes I understand. The rest are varying ones from

Sara getting more and more frantic. I check the time; I've been gone for roughly four hours. In the last message she's threatening to phone the police. She is such a drama queen. I sigh and scroll through to her name and press call. I don't want the police out looking for me, after all.

'Alma, thank fuck for that. Where the hell have you been? I've been looking for you everywhere.' Sara's voice is shrill and breathy and I can tell she's worried, she's normally so calm and collected.

'Oh, um sorry. I didn't mean to make you worry,' I say feeling awful. 'My phone was flat.' I should have thought, we're in an unfamiliar town and we don't know anyone. I'd have been so worried about her if she'd gone off and not been in touch. At least she doesn't seem so angry with me anymore and her concern shows me we're still friends even if I have been a bit of a dick.

'It's okay,' she says, her tone relaxing. 'Where are you now?'

'I'm back at the hotel,' I reply sheepishly. 'Sitting in Reception, borrowing their charger which I'm not allowed to waltz off with.'

Sara laughs, I can practically hear her rolling her eyes on the phone. 'Okay, wait there. I'll be with you in fifteen. Please don't tell me you've been there for ages?' she asks, her voice becoming warmer and more like her usual self.

'Nope, just got here.'

'Good. Otherwise I'll be having words with the front desk. I asked them to call me if you turned up. Not that they have,' she says, sounding annoyed. 'I've been wandering around the streets searching for you.'

'Oh, I'm so sorry…' I start but Sara cuts me off.

'You're back now. It's fine, it was only the last hour I started to get *really* concerned.' She rings off and I slump against the back of the chair, running everything through my mind again. Sara isn't going to believe any of this.

Thirty minutes later Sara bowls through into Reception with three shopping bags in tow, her clothes and hair in disarray. She drops the bags on the floor beside me and drags a chair across from the other side of the reception area, much to the obvious irritation of the receptionist, but he says nothing, perhaps he can tell it wouldn't be wise to mess with Sara.

'So where have you been this whole time?' she asks with her hands on her hips. She's trying to feign anger but I can tell she's pleased to see me.

'I was in the outlet, mostly at the fountain,' I explain.

'Oh really?' she cuts in before I can tell her anymore. 'I was in the outlet all afternoon.' She frowns, clearly trying to work out why she didn't see me. I wonder if she wandered past when I was mid-confrontation. No, she wouldn't have missed that spectacle.

'I can see that. And here I was thinking you were out searching for me this whole time,' I say offering a small smile and nodding at her shopping bags. It feels good to be with Sara again. She's lifted my mood back up already. Even if Denise and Jenna have gone.

'I was looking for you in the shops. It's not my fault they also had amazing sales on.' She grins. 'You know Jenna and Denise have gone home?'

'I know. It's all my fault. I feel bad about Jenna,' I say quietly, hoping she'll say it wasn't too bad.

'You should,' Sara says firmly. Well that's me told.

'Yes,' I say in a small voice. I feel quite ashamed now. 'Although I think it was a slight overreaction on

Jenna's part,' I add grasping at straws. I hope Sara will validate my thoughts and make me feel better about how I reacted to Jenna.

'No.' Sara is never one to mince her words. 'You were in the wrong. I'm sorry, you know I love you but what you did was nasty. If I can't tell you that then what kind of friend am I? I know you've had a lot going on with the Nick thing but have you tried to talk to Jenna about what's going on in *her* life?'

'What do you mean what's going on in her life? I already know it's perfect. Perfect husband. Perfect kids. Everything is wonderful. Perfect husband just got a promotion yadda yadda,' I say dismissively. I'm so bored with it all. Everything is always perfect for Jenna.

'Oh, Alma, you really have had your head in the sand. Have you not wondered why Jenna is over at your Mum's so often? *I* don't know what's going on and I don't know her that well but even I can see that something isn't right. I didn't realise you were so imperceptive. She's your sister. You should be there for her. Did you not see her crying when we went to the club? You need to talk to her.'

Was she? I think back to that night and remember her and Denise going to the toilets for a long time. I thought the look on her face when they returned was irritation but it could quite easily have been something else. Why am I so out of tune with my own sister? I suddenly start to think about how self-involved I've been recently. Wallowing in my own self-pity, fed up with my job and life in general, trying to forget about Nick, obsessing about Nick. What did I miss?

I think back over the last few months. Jenna has increasingly come over to Mum and Dad's but I never really thought much of it. She's always been close with

Mum and always seemed to have a reason for visiting. With Dave's promotion in the works, as she never stopped reminding me, and the kids off with friends, she liked the company. It all made perfect sense at the time. Nothing out of the ordinary.

Sara watches me and sighs. 'Look you need to talk to Jenna and you owe her a huge apology for that outburst. That was cruel and humiliating. I felt embarrassed for the poor girl. Also, for the record I did want her on this trip so it wasn't even true that no one wanted her here. I asked her to come along specifically, I thought she seemed like she needed it as much as you.'

I hang my head in shame. I'm the worst sister. It's all so clear now something *is* going on with Jenna. She is acting strangely. I don't know why I was so blind to it. My own jealously and assumptions about her life have clouded my judgement. Why didn't she just tell me though? I'd have been there for her if she said something was up. I resolve to be a better sister and find out what's going on. I have definitely got some grovelling to do, I don't think an apology note slipped under her bedroom door like when we were kids will cut it now. I need to see her in person.

I fill Sara in about bumping into Nick and the revelation about Kelly and the baby. Sara sits there with her hand over her mouth the entire time, her eyes wide and shocked.

'Fucking bitch,' she says. 'I can't get over the cheek of it all and the pure gutlessness of him. Why not just admit it? Why not just dump you properly?'

'God knows,' I say. 'They didn't want to be the bad guys, I suppose. Didn't want all our friends on the ship to know they were horrible people. Didn't want the confrontation. They're both pathetic and I'm glad they're out of my life. I finally got the closure I needed.'

'Yes, you did. I *knew* this was a good idea.' Sara has a smug look on her face, so pleased her plans have all come to fruition. 'I just wish I could have been there and seen their gawping faces. Especially when you threw the smoothies over him. Whatever made you do that?'

'I don't know. Maybe I was channelling my inner you.' I laugh.

'No, darling, you were channelling your true self and you deserve much better than that prick.' Never one to mince her words Sara continues, 'Were you dressed like *that?* Never mind. You stuck it to him anyway. Well done you.'

'Thanks for that, I know I look a mess.' I roll my eyes but I'm still too pleased with myself for standing up to them to be bothered about how I look.

Now I really need to get back to Twinton and face the music. This trip has been a real eye opener, one that has really made me look at my life and I need to make some changes. I'm keen to get started and get my life back on track. I just want to be home. I'm sick of being taken for granted at work and I hate my job. I miss photography. After my degree it took me a while to find my feet in the photography world and I took a job in Holborns while I planned my future. It felt like all my dreams had come true when I got the job as a cruise ship photographer. It seemed so glamorous.

Boy was I wrong about the glamour but the experience improved my photography skills no end. I'm so sad that I've let it go by the wayside. It's so rare that I get my kit out anymore. I think of my cameras lying in the box under my bed, unused. It's such a waste. I need to get back into it and rediscover my passion. Going back to Holborns with my tail between my legs after Nick ghosted me was utterly humiliating and I don't know why I did it, I'm sure I could have found something else if I'd really tried. It would feel so good to leave that awful job. Once and for all.

I think about whether I'm ready to find someone else. Although I'm really not too sure about internet dating after the Lewis the Loo Loser incident. An image of Lewis with chocolate ice cream sliding down his face pops into my head and I smile, he totally had it coming. This whole journey has made me think about my worth and I'm worth so much more than that. I deserve so much better and I'm not going to settle for anything less.

I can't wait to get back and start my life over.

Chapter 14

It takes Sara and me five and a half hours and three different trains to get home to Twinton. At least we don't have our bags to drag with us, they're in Jenna's car, other than Sara's shopping of course. During the journey I really do regret how I treated Jenna. After all, she didn't have to give up time with her family to come on this trip. I'm also really eager to know what's been going on. Sara is being quite tight lipped and I'm unsure if it's because she doesn't know anything or because she's being loyal to Jenna. I can't really argue with either reason and I feel like a complete shit about it.

I'm wondering if Denise is pissed off with me as well. I've not heard from her since they arrived home, which must be hours ago and we normally message each other frequently. It's not really in her character to hold a grudge but I hate the thought of her being mad with me too. I feel like a naughty school child, this must be what it's like to be in her class. I always imagined her to be a soft touch but the thought of disappointing her is awful. If her pupils feel like this, they must all be very well behaved.

'Penny for them,' Sara asks.

I've been silent most of the journey back, using the time to reflect and let everything sink in. We're in the taxi on the way back to our homes now.

'I'm still getting my head around the whole Kelly and Nick thing. I'm glad I know now but the deceit is hard to swallow,' I say. 'I'm also feeling quite bad about Jenna,' I add sheepishly, hoping Sara isn't going to make me feel any worse.

'Aw I know,' she says rubbing my shoulder. 'Kelly and Nick are dicks. And you *should* feel bad about Jenna,' she says. I let my shoulders slump. 'But you can make amends.'

'Do you think Denise is mad at me too?' I probe hoping she can make me feel better.

'No, I don't think so?' She raises her eyebrows making it a question.

'It's just she's not really spoken to me since she got back,' I admit. 'And that's not like her at all.'

'Well everyone has something going on in their lives too. She's probably just spending time with Jay.'

I'm starting to think I might be a bit of a bad friend. I'm not overly sure what is going on in Denise's life, if anything. I've not paid much attention. I've mainly wallowed in my own misfortunes. I resolve to find out and make sure we're okay when I get home.

It's gone 8.30pm by the time I get home. I shuffle into the house with my bags in my arms and dump them all by the door. I don't have the energy to pull them up the stairs.

'Good time love?' Mum asks.

'Oh, um yeah. I'm just going to go lie down. Long journey.' I skulk past her and rush for the safety of my bedroom. I think about phoning Jenna or Denise but I decide not to. Best to leave them for tonight. I'll try to make amends tomorrow, perhaps if they sleep on it things won't be so bad. I wince at the thought of the tears streaming down Jenna's face. Oh why did I have to shout at her? I wish I had Denise's calm demeanour, I bet she never shouts at Jay.

Dad knocks and enters the room and brings in my bags. Such a gentleman, although he probably hated the clutter and mess in the hallway.

'Thank you.' I give him my brightest smile

'No worries love. I hope you're okay,' he says lifting his eyebrows at me. I can tell he's concerned but he won't push it any further.

'I'm okay. Don't worry Dad,' I reassure him.

He pops the bags down in the corner of my room and leaves me to it.

I lie on my bed and think about unpacking, finally deciding it's just too much effort. A lot has happened over the past three days and I don't know if I've fully digested everything. I could really do with someone to talk to but Sara has just got home and I'm not sure if Denise is talking to me. Anyway, maybe Sara is right and Denise just wants to spend time with Jay. Not everything's about me.

Mum taps on the door before entering and I look over at her expectantly.

'Why don't you come down and have some food?' she asks. Why are Mums some kind of homing device? They just know when you need something.

A round of cheese on toast later and I've regaled her with the whole sorry tale, even Lewis the Loo Loser.

She was in hysterics when I told her about the ice cream incident. The only detail I do leave out is Jenna. I already feel bad enough about the whole situation and I don't want Mum making me feel worse. Or worse still, worrying about Jenna.

'I just can't believe that Nick the Prick, is that what you call him, did that?' I stifle a giggle at my oh so proper mother swearing. 'He doesn't sound anywhere near good enough for you, sweetheart. You're better off without him.'

She's fetched some chocolates from the top shelf and silently laid them on the island in front of me. I grab one and stuff it in my mouth.

'I must say I am a little confused though,' she continues. 'I thought you dumped him, or it was a mutual decision?'

I told everyone that I'd finished with him or that we'd grown apart when I came home. I didn't want the endless questions so I pretended that it was my decision and I was happy about it. It was difficult at the time to keep a brave face on it but I couldn't bear the embarrassment of them knowing the truth and asking why. Especially when I didn't even know why myself.

'Hmmm, well I think I was a bit embarrassed,' I reply before stuffing another chocolate in my face. I'm tired of the whole sorry affair and I've had enough of talking about it this evening. 'Is there anything going on with Jenna?' I ask Mum, changing the subject and searching her face for any tells.

'Oh, I don't know but she has been around a lot more than usual. I've noticed that. Although I thought it was because you two were finally getting along again which has been nice.' She gives me one of those knowing Mum looks.

I hadn't even realised Mum had seen us pull apart over time. I'd just thought it had been so gradual, but she's right we were once thick as thieves. I begin to wonder how it has all affected Jenna. Before I went away on the ship we were still pretty close, we'd been apart while I was at university but we kept each other in the loop about our lives. She even threw me a going away party when I got my ship job. She was my biggest advocate. I remember how excited she was at the prospect of meeting Nick. I think that's what made it all the worse when I came back with my tail between my legs, boyfriendless and jobless. That's why I shut her out so completely. I looked at her life and decided it was too perfect and my insane jealousy meant I couldn't bring myself to tell her the truth.

But the grass isn't always greener. Apparently.

'Oh well yes, we have been getting on well.' I wince at the lie but hope that I can turn it around. 'I just noticed that she's not been quite herself lately.'

'Well, you know it's not always the easiest being a Mum. I know Sam and Claire are at that difficult age at the moment and it's hard when your children pull away from you. It can make you feel a bit surplus to requirements.' She nods and I get the feeling she isn't just talking about Jenna anymore.

Since leaving the ship I have distanced myself from everyone and hidden my feelings about Nick. It's been really nice confiding in Mum like this and I don't know why I felt the need to hide this from her. I really need to take control of my life and speak to Jenna. Where do I start?

Chapter 15

I can't face the thought of work in the morning so I call Liz and explain that I'm still not feeling quite right. Over the phone I can hear the squelch of her sanitizer as she squirts it into her hands, as if she could catch my illness through the receiver. I bet she'll need to clean her whole desk after this conversation. I go into graphic detail about how poorly I've been and I can hear her almost gagging. I know this is an easy way to get her off the phone as quickly as possible. She ends the call as soon as she can and tells me to just message her if I'm off tomorrow but if I'm off Monday I'll need a doctor's note. I won't be off Monday. After all, apart from going through the wringer on a personal level there's nothing actually wrong with me.

I do have a new outlook on life though and I feel determined to get everything in order. Start afresh. I decide to write a list of the things I want and need to do.

1. Jenna – make amends top priority.
2. Denise – find out if I need to make amends and

make amends.

3. Job – find something more enjoyable. Get back into photography? At least quit this job. It's just depressing.
4. Move out – find somewhere cheap, but nice.
5. Wardrobe – everyone seems to think I dress terribly – must sort, perhaps make a bit more effort with my appearance in general. Have I let myself slip?
6. Dating – go on another date – surely I've had my share of pricks and losers now and am due a good one? Right?

I already start to feel better about everything although I can't help but wince every time I read the first item on my list. This list is just the beginning, I'm going to turn my life around. I'm going to take control. I want more for myself now. I shouldn't have let a little heartache take away all of my passion and confidence.

I open up my laptop and start to look through my photographs from the cruise ship. There are all sorts of landscapes from my times in ports, some portraits of friends and wedding photos. I baulk just thinking of all the people I cut off after I left the ship. It really is a shame I'm not in touch with any of them anymore. They were my life, my friends, my family, my colleagues, when I was on board. No one understands the stresses, strains and delights of ship life better than they do. We have that common bond but I threw it away because of Nick. I should have given them more credit and told them what was going on. I can't help but think of the irony that the only friend I kept in touch with was Kelly because she knew what had happened. Little did I know how she betrayed me. I resolve to add another item to my list.

7. Reconnect with my ship friends (obv not Kelly!)

Keen to get started, I fire off a load of emails to everyone asking where they are and what they're up to and apologising for not getting in touch sooner. I explain how embarrassed I was when Nick broke up with me and ask them to forgive me. I don't mention that Kelly and Nick now have a baby. I don't want to talk about them anymore and it would only raise more questions. I idly wonder if any of them knew, I hope they would have told me. I happily tick item seven off my list feeling pleased that I've made a start. I go to close my laptop but see an instant message ping up, it's Lynette; we worked together on the ship in the photography department. I always had the feeling she wasn't that fussed on Nick because she really tried to persuade me to stay when I told everyone I wasn't going to work another contract. She said it was crazy as we'd not been together long and I was giving up the opportunity of a life time. But I was determined to leave and start my life with Nick.

Lynette: Hey stranger, long time no speak. It's good to hear from you.
Alma: Hi, it's good to hear from you too. How are you?
Lynette: Good, still on the ships, busy, busy as usual. Sorry to hear about you and Nick.
Alma: Thank you, how is it going?
Lynette: Just about to go on out for the Caribbean season, we're a photographer short you know.
Alma: Really? I don't think I could come back.

Lynette: Why not? At least think about it. I'm sure they'd have you back. You were amazing, especially your wedding shots.

Alma: Thank you ☺

Lynette: You were always too good for Nick anyway, that's a nasty thing he did to ignore you and not just break up with you. I did wonder why you didn't respond to my messages but just figured you were too busy with land life.

Alma: Thanks Lynette and I'm sorry for not getting in touch sooner, I was so embarrassed about the whole situation.

I appreciate that she didn't take the opportunity to rub it in or say she was right about Nick. She never actually said she didn't like him but it was always a feeling I had. I never thought too much of it. I bite the bullet and decide to tell her about Nick and Kelly. I have to know if everyone was laughing at me behind my back. If everyone did know, I'm not sure I'd be able to forgive them.

Alma: Nick had a fling with Kelly behind my back and they have a baby together now. Did you know?

Lynette: OMG what? No. I did not know. He's still in touch with some of the guys so I did kind of know you two weren't together, but not the details. No one has ever mentioned Kelly. Or a baby?! I thought she was cruising around Australia. I'm sure no one else knows because you know what gossip is like on this ship and I haven't heard a word.

Alma: That makes me feel so much better. I thought he really liked me.

Lynette: I thought he liked you too.

Alma: Really? I always had the impression you didn't like him.

Lynette: Well, I just thought he was a little smarmy, but I didn't want to say anything because you obviously liked each other. He just wasn't my cup of tea, a bit arrogant, you know. And, he changed you when you were with him. You weren't the same after you two became official. He always seemed to be holding you back and telling you what to do.

I think back over our relationship, over all the memories we shared together. I've run it all through my mind countless times. It's as though the rose-tinted glasses have finally fallen off and I can see all the times *he* decided what we were going to do in port, and how he monopolised my time. For some reason he didn't like me hanging around with the gang so I began to limit the time I spent with them outside of work. Lynette's right it was all on his terms. How blind I was, but the blinkers are off now.

Alma: I never really thought about it like that. Anyway, I'm happy without him.

Lynette: Good for you. What are you up to nowadays, anything good?

Alma: Nothing good right now, but I will be.

Still hyped up from my exchange with Lynette and ready to get through my list I fire off a message to Denise apologising for my behaviour towards Jenna. I tell her I hope there are no bad feelings between the two of us and I'd love to catch up with her and tell her about when I bumped into Nick the Prick again.

Denise: Hey, no worries, we're okay. Sorry not been in touch. It was all a bit much and I didn't know what to say. Thank you for apologising. Have you had a chance to speak to Jenna yet?

Denise: Oh and you spoke to Nick??

Alma: Not spoken to Jenna yet but I'll go over and speak to her soon. Yes, I bumped into him. It's a long story. Come over later for a chat?

Denise: Okay, be over about 7?

Alma: Perfect.

1. Jenna – make amends top priority.
2. ~~Denise – find out if I need to make amends and make amends.~~
3. Job – find something more enjoyable. Get back into photography? At least quit this job. It's just depressing.
4. Move out – find somewhere cheap, but nice.
5. Wardrobe – everyone seems to think I dress terribly – must sort.
6. Dating – go on another date – surely I've had my share of pricks and losers now and am due a good one? Right?
7. ~~Reconnect with my ship friends (obv not Kelly!)~~

Now that's two things crossed off my list. I have a feeling the others won't be quite so easy to cross off. I bite the bullet and call Jenna; it rings and rings but she doesn't answer. I guess I deserve that. I'm going to have to go over there in person. I try her again on the off chance and promise myself if she doesn't answer I'll go immediately. It goes straight to voicemail which tells me everything I need to know about how mad Jenna is with me. This is going to take some serious grovelling.

I head downstairs, grab my coat and jump in the car and drive over to Jenna's house. I knock loudly on her front door and keep my finger pressed on the bell button to make sure she answers because I don't want to give myself any excuse to leave. Jenna opens the door after a few moments and I'm shocked at how upset she looks. I feel awful now, I must have really got to her.

'What do you want?' she croaks, only keeping the door open a crack and ready to close it at any given second. I stick my foot out so she doesn't get the chance, this is fast becoming one of my little tricks.

'Look, I'm really sorry, I didn't mean to upset you. Can I come in and have a chat?' I step forward so it's difficult for her to say no but I can see she's reluctant.

She must be home alone now; Dave will be at work and the kids at school. She shrugs and opens the door, defeated. When I come in I can see she's still in her pyjamas and the house is a mess. This is not like Jenna; her car may well be a state but her home is normally spotless. She's been away for a few days so has a bit of catching up to do but I'm shocked to see it like this. Jenna notices me looking around the room.

'Excuse the mess. Wasn't expecting visitors,' she says flatly, shrugging her shoulders and dragging her feet into the living room.

'Oh um, that's okay. Sorry.' I feel awkward, uncomfortable, as though I'm trespassing.

We go into the living room and sit on separate sofas. She doesn't even offer me a drink which again is not like Jenna, but I suppose she is cross with me and doesn't really want me here at all.

We sit together, an uncomfortable silence filling the air, finally I can't take it anymore.

'I'm sorry, please forgive me,' I beg. 'I was reeling from the whole Nick thing and I took it out on you because that's what sisters do and that was wrong. Please can you forgive me? I am so, so sorry. Of course I wanted you there. I don't know why I said that.' I look into her eyes trying to show her how sincere I am.

'You seemed pretty sure when you said it,' she responds quietly, looking at the floor. 'You humiliated me in front of your friends.'

'I know and I'm really sorry for that too. What do I need to do to make it up to you?' I plead.

'It's fine.' But it really doesn't look fine and as I watch her she starts to crumble, her shoulders heaving up and down and silent tears streaming down her face. I am genuinely sorry but I'm starting to think this isn't just about me.

'Are you okay? Is there something else going on?' I venture trying to catch her eye.

Jenna mumbles something under her breath but I don't quite catch it.

'Pardon?'

'I… think… Dave… is…. having…. an…. affair,' she finally squeaks between sobs.

'What?' I'm shocked. Dave is the perfect man, the perfect husband and father. How can this be? Surely not.

'He's always in the office, working late. I know the drill; it's happened to a few of my friends. And look at you and Nick the Prick, all men are at it,' she spits between sobs. This just doesn't feel right to me. I may find it annoying how perfect he is but he's a genuinely decent guy. If he is having an affair there's no hope for anyone.

Then it all comes pouring out in one long ramble.

'And the kids hate me, they don't need me anymore. I'm just a glorified taxi and maid. I feel like I don't even know who I am anymore. I don't even have a job. I took time off of work to raise my children and they're not interested in me anymore and Dave is never here. I feel so lonely.'

'So have you actually caught him cheating?' I ask.

'Well, no but you just know, don't you?' She dismisses me with a wave of her hand.

'Have you heard something or seen some messages?' What a dog, I can't believe this. I frown and rub my hands over my face.

'Um, no. But he works late every night. He's never here and even when he is he's always going off to have private chats on his phone for ages. He always leaves the room. I'm not stupid,' she sobs.

'Didn't he just get a promotion?' I'm baffled. She's just going on a feeling. No proof.

'Yes, but I know he is.'

'Have you asked him?'

'Not yet, I haven't got the nerve. I'm not ready for him to leave me. I love him. If I confront him, it means it's over, doesn't it? We've been together for ever, what will I do?'

She looks pleadingly at me, wanting answers to these impossible questions. It seems absolutely crazy that she's convinced herself he's cheating just because she has a *feeling* but isn't that what all women who find out say? That they just knew? Women's intuition. I'm obviously lacking in that area because I had no idea Nick was having an affair. Something still doesn't feel right.

'Have you considered that he isn't having an affair?' I say softly, trying to tread lightly.

'I know he is; I know him. Something is going on. He's really off with me. We never have sex,' Jenna whines.

'Then let's go find out,' I say. She's helped me on my crazy trip and now I can help her. This is the perfect way for me to make up for what I said to her, for hurting her. 'Is he working late tonight?'

'He works late every night!' she wails and puts her face in her hands.

'Looks like we need to do a bit of good old-fashioned stalking. Good news is that we happen to be experts at that.' That comment at least raises a smile from her.

I move over next to her and put my arm around my sister. She's a lot more sensitive than she lets on. I feel disgusted with myself that I've not been here for her. Her problems, real or imagined, are far worse than mine. I resolve to be a better sister and try much harder.

'Come on,' I say, giving her shoulder a squeeze. 'Get some clothes on and let's go and find out one way or another.'

Watch   out   Dave,   here   we   come.

Chapter 16

Later that evening and after a quick call to Denise and Sara, we're all dressed in black and wearing some wigs from Claire's dressing up box. Claire has had some of the dressing up stuff since she was a little girl and we all look ridiculous. Fortunately, Claire and Sam are ensconced in their bedrooms and not even aware of what we're doing.

Denise is driving as Dave would recognise Jenna's car and we can't have that. We drive around to his office and park outside and wait. His car is there so it certainly looks promising; he's still at work. The snacks this time round have been well thought out. As we sit in the car it occurs to me that we've thought a lot more about them than what we're actually doing and what it might mean. We sit here watching his car for the next half hour, eating ourselves silly and dishing out a few wines for those of us not driving. We see the odd person come in or out of the office but not much else is going on.

'So if he stays there then comes home at the end, then what?' Sara asks. 'This seems a bit silly to me. Why don't you just confront him?' Sara would be the first to have it out with any boyfriend, never being one to shy away from a fight.

'He'll deny it, I know it. I know he's cheating. I can't explain it, I just know. Women's intuition. I can feel him pulling away from me,' Jenna says as Denise nods along.

Whilst we wait, I fill in Denise and Jenna on everything that happened with Nick and Kelly. They are stunned to say the least but they love that I threw his smoothies all over him. Even if I did look like a scruffy bum in the process. Retelling it makes me enjoy the feeling of satisfaction and closure all over again.

That reminds me and I take a furtive look at my list. I can scratch off Jenna because I'm definitely being supportive over this, but there are a few others the girls may be able to help me with.

'What's that you've got there?' Jenna asks peering over my shoulder and trying to grab at the list.

'Oh, just a list. I'm trying to get my life on track, you know.' I shrug, feeling embarrassed by it in written form.

'Oh.' She rubs her hands together. 'This sounds like something fun to pass the time. Let's have a look, let's see what made the list.'

I don't hand it over, but I do read it out. Denise looks at me in surprise when she hears her name on there, then reassures me that we're fine. Sara offers to take me out shopping and also says she is having a bit of a clear out so if I'm interested she'd be happy for me to have some of her clothes. I'm thrilled about this. I don't think I could really afford to buy a whole new wardrobe but I'm sure I could find some things that are hopefully not too *out there* in her wardrobes.

'If you want to get out from under your Mum and Dad's feet why don't you come and stay with me for a while? Until you find something more suitable?' Sara suggests. 'After all, I do have a spare room.'

I'm astonished; this is unprecedented for Sara. Since moving out of her parents' home she has always lived alone and loved it that way. For her to offer this has really touched me, I can feel my eyes begin to fill with tears. She's such a good friend to me. She's never even allowed a man to move in, a few of them have tried but those ones were swiftly dumped.

'Are you sure?' I look into her eyes, giving her a chance to take it back but willing her not to.

'Well I wouldn't be offering if I wasn't. It'll help me out with the mortgage anyway,' she says dismissively. 'It's only a temporary thing mind, but I think it'd be good for you…' she pauses, 'And maybe me,' she adds.

'Good for you?' I ask wondering what she could mean, she's always loved living alone.

'I've not lived with anyone for a long time. I've been thinking recently it would be nice to have someone and even to maybe live with them. Mick is pretty nice.'

I raise my eyebrows in surprise, whilst I've had my head in the sand what else have I missed. Mick? Who's Mick?

'Who's Mick?'

'Oh, just someone I've been seeing.'

'But you got off with Hulk when we were away.'

'It's not serious or anything but I'm not ruling it out.' Sara grins.

I'm so shocked but I see Denise and Jenna exchange a look, so they've already heard of Mick. Am I the only one out of the loop? I feel bad; I seem to have missed what's going on in everyone's life at the moment. Am I really so self-obsessed? I stare down at the list in my lap, so there's another two I can cross off but I think there's something else I need to add.

1. ~~Jenna – make amends top priority.~~
2. ~~Denise – find out if I need to make amends and make amends.~~
3. Job – find something more enjoyable. Get back into photography? At least quit this job. It's just depressing.
4. ~~Move out – find somewhere cheap, but nice.~~
5. Wardrobe – everyone seems to think I dress terribly – must sort.
6. Dating – go on another date – surely I've had my share of pricks and losers now and am due a good one? Right?
7. ~~Reconnect with my ship friends (obv not Kelly!)~~
8. Be a better friend – don't be so selfish. Find out what's going on in my friends' lives.

Jenna laughs when she reads the addition to my list over my shoulder as I write it. 'Oh Alma, you're not that bad. I think it's probably more us not telling you because we could see you had enough to deal with,' she reassures me.

That makes sense, sort of. I start to feel a little better. Unless Jenna is just being kind.

'She right,' adds Sara. 'I didn't tell you about Mick because I didn't want to rub it in. I was going to tell you after your date with Lewis but then it went terribly wrong for you and that just wasn't the right time. We've only been dating a short time but I do really like him. It really made me realise when I was getting with Hulk, I felt awful. We're not exclusive but I'm thinking of seeing what he thinks.'

I think back to that night, I remember thinking it was odd that she didn't go home with Hulk. She must really like this Mick guy. I smile at Sara; it is lovely to hear that she's happy with a man.

'Just because everything isn't perfect in my life doesn't mean I don't want to hear about yours.' I look around at all of my friends. 'That goes for all of you. Good or bad, you don't have to protect me, I'm your friend too and *I* want to be there for *you*.'

'Let's agree we'll tell each other what's going on more,' Denise says, making the peace.

Sara raises her cup. 'Agreed. Now I need a good drink, especially if I'm going to be living with this one.' She smiles broadly over at me as she tips more wine into her cup.

I scribble number eight off of my list, I think I can do this without having it written down. It's something you continuously do anyway so when would I ever be able to put a line through it? Just dating and a nice new job are left on my list now.

'I could set you up,' starts Denise, referring to item six. I know a really nice guy.'

'No, no I think that one can wait. I really want to concentrate on a job first. I want to be able to meet someone and feel pride in who I am and what I do. Not embarrassed that I'm in a dead-end job at Holborns.'

The girls all smile and agree. It's nice they're not fighting me this time.

'Look, look is that him?' Sara points, drawing our attention back to the task at hand. Jenna showed everyone a picture of him when we got into the car so they could see the *suspect*. We've had a few instances where the wrong person has been pointed out but this time it really is Dave.

'Yes, that's him. Oh God, where do you think he's going?' It's only seven o'clock and he said he won't be home until ten or later.'

We wait until he climbs into his car and then Denise starts the engine and we follow him out of the car park.

After a short journey he parks outside a fancy restaurant and goes inside. Jenna is visibly hunched up and I can feel the atmosphere in the car, tense and brittle. I look at her face and I can see what she's thinking. This looks neither good nor promising. She looks worried. Maybe she's right and Dave is cheating on her, but I really hope not. It just doesn't seem like the Dave that I know.

Fortunately, he sits at a table for two in the window. Our view is slightly obscured by the window frame but we should be able to see whoever he is meeting. Fifteen minutes goes by and then a very attractive blonde woman approaches his table. He stands and disappears behind the window frame for a second or two, presumably helping her with her coat.

Then he reappears and we watch as they greet each other, hugs and kisses on cheeks. That's not normal is it? I don't greet anyone I work with like that. Then they sit down and have an animated conversation while the waiter hovers to take their order. The tension in the car is palpable, to say the least. No one knows what to say and the longer it goes on the more awkward it gets.

Attractive blonde is sitting next to Dave facing outwards towards us, Dave is facing inwards next to the window. We can only see his side profile or the back of his head when he speaks to her. We can see her face really well though. Oh, her beautiful face and elegant hand gestures, laughing and touching her long blonde hair. Touching her hair? Isn't that a flirting thing, an unconscious way of saying you like someone? Come to think of it his knees are crossed towards her, isn't that another? I'm no body language expert but this does not look good for Jenna. Watching the whole scenario is excruciating.

Now Dave is laughing and smiling, his head turning towards us. They order drinks and we see some fancy looking concoctions that look like cocktails come out. Who drinks on a business dinner? And if you do, wouldn't it just be the wine to keep within budget, not cocktails surely. I chance a look at Jenna, her face has fallen and she looks devastated. I know she suspected this but I'm witnessing the moment it has been confirmed. The worst moment of her life.

Now I feel awful for shutting her out and not being there for her. For being a terrible sister. I resolve to be there for her throughout this, get her through, dare I think it, divorce. If it comes to that, I can be there. Where else could it go? Forgiveness? Things will never be the same for Jenna now because what we've just seen can never be unseen. You can forgive but you can never really forget something of this magnitude. This is the moment when everything went wrong, when Jenna has realised that her life is a lie. My heart breaks for her. Here I am talking about myself again, trying to improve my life and hers is falling apart. I am a selfish cow. I put my arm out to Jenna and touch her gently.

Jenna puts her face in her hands, shrugging off my gesture and finally breaks the silence. 'I knew it, I just knew it.' She starts to sob uncontrollably.

'You don't know anything,' Denise sooths. 'She could be anyone. Maybe she's a client or a friend,' she adds, grasping at straws, but we all saw her and the way he greeted her. This looks like more than a business dinner. It's so intimate, just the two of them.

'Go and find out,' Sara says forcefully. She's bored with all of this now and wants it to be done. If it was her, she would have asked him outright, being direct is definitely her forte.

Jenna looks at her as though she must be joking and shakes her head slowly.

'I'm not kidding, go in there right now and find out what the hell is going on. You're his wife, you have a right to know.'

Jenna shakes her head more now. 'I can't. I'm too ashamed. I can't cause a scene in that nice restaurant. The wronged wife shouting at her cheating husband. I just can't do it,' she says. 'I won't,' she adds, looking determined. I don't think she'll be so easily convinced to take action, unlike me.

'What do you have to be ashamed about? It's him, not you. Go in there or I will and I mean it.' Sara and the tough love again.

I look over at Jenna. 'She means it you know,' I say.

'Don't be ridiculous what would I even say?' She cries more and the tears stream down her face.

'How about, "You were supposed to be at work, you fucking arsehole," or "Who the fuck is this? What's going on?" Any one of those.'

Jenna wipes her tears and visibly straightens. In that moment I can feel her pulling herself together, pulling everything inwards. Her face hardens and takes on a look of determination.

'Take me home,' she says through gritted teeth.

'Are you sure...' I begin but Jenna cuts me off.

'Now!' she shouts.

Sara and Denise are noticeably shocked, Jenna isn't the type to shout but she has busted out her Mum voice. The one I've heard her use when the kids were little and taking forever to do even the littlest of tasks. They both look at me for guidance. It's *her* husband and *her* choice. I'm here supporting her now and if she wants to talk to him later about it, I think that's fair enough. If she doesn't fancy a public showdown, who am I to judge? It may not have been the way I would have liked it with Nick but this is far more serious. This is Jenna's husband. My brother-in-law. There are kids involved. I thought he was perfect, how wrong was I?

'Let's go,' I confirm in a small voice, resolved to follow Jenna's lead.

The journey is tense, Jenna spends the whole drive staring out of the window in silence and no one dares say a word after the shouting. When we get back to her house, I begin to get ready to get out of the car with Jenna. I think some sister time would be good right now.

'I want to be alone.' Jenna looks pointedly at me.

Okay, hint taken. 'Are you sure?' I venture, I'm being supportive so I don't want to push her. 'Is there anything we can do, anything *I* can do?'

With this she looks up at everyone. It's evident from the mascara all over her face that she's cried even more on the journey home, her face to the window. She composes herself and replies. 'Yes, you can all forget what you saw tonight. I don't want to discuss it. Ever.' She looks around us all. 'Is that clear?'

There are so many questions hanging in the air. Is she not going to confront him? Or does she just want to deal with this quietly? Is she going to let him get away with it and pretend she doesn't know? I'm feeling really confused but I can sense from her tone and the look she is giving us that this isn't up for discussion. Without waiting for a response she pushes the door open, gets out and walks up the drive to her house leaving Sara, Denise and I gaping like goldfish. I thought she had the perfect husband, the perfect life.

But I was wrong.

Chapter 17

3 months later

'So, tonight's the big night. How're you feeling?' Jenna's eyes flash and she gives me a big grin.

'A bit nervous, you know it's been a while. It feels good to get all the equipment out again though. I know once I start I'll get into the zone, just like on the ship. I've photographed loads of portraits and events like this. I know what I'm doing,' I say as much to reassure myself as Jenna.

'Equipment out again? I've hardly seen you without your camera for the last few months,' Jenna laughs. She's right, I've taken every opportunity to take as many photographs as possible, it's been a lovely spring leading into summer and I've loved being outside and using my kit again.

'I know, but it's both cameras and all the lenses and renting out the studio equipment. It's on a bigger scale. Not just pottering around Twinton taking photos or photographing my mates,' I explain, the nerves rising up in my stomach. I feel like a novice all over again.

'So what is it you need me to do?' Jenna checks.

Jenna has agreed to be my assistant for the night which is really kind and supportive of her.

'Mainly helping with the set up and organising the people waiting for their photographs. I might also get you to take a few photos. I'll set the camera up so you don't need to worry. Do you think you'll be okay to do that? It'll be good to see how you get on. We need candid photos as everyone is walking around, looking at animals, playing games, that sort of thing. It doesn't matter if they're not good as I just won't include them in the edit.' Jenna has been surprisingly keen and helpful. Suggesting where we could set up the equipment, going between Dave and me and making sure I'm looked after for the whole night. I'm even included in the dinner and they've said when I've finished I can stay and enjoy the drinks they've put on but I know I'll probably just want to go back and look at my photographs.

Despite being a cheating arsehole Dave has pulled it out of the bag. He got me this job, a proper paid photography job, photographing his work's summer event. They're having it at the zoo which seems ludicrous to me, but each to their own. Everyone gets to have a look around the animals, there are games on the big lawn where people normally picnic when visiting and a disco in the evening inside the zoo café.

I'll have my portrait equipment set up for people to come over and have photos with me over the evening. I have some fun summery props and I'll create a border to show they're from the summer event at Stanis.

Their employee care is far greater than what I'm used to. In Holborns we're lucky if they'll pay for a Christmas meal, never mind a summer event. I guess these big companies who have everyone working 70-

hour weeks have to give some benefits – aside from the obscene amount of money Dave gets paid – and the budget for this is huge. They always have a professional photographer and they're going the whole hog having me. I've not charged too much for my time but I have budgeted it so I can rent some lighting equipment and a back drop. I've made myself some business cards and I'm hoping that I can get some other photography work from this.

After all, this is a big company, there must be employees who want some family or wedding photos. I've created a Facebook page with some of the portraits that I've taken of various friends and their families so people can look me up and see my work. I'm really trying to build my portfolio although unfortunately I can't use any of the photographs from the ship as the copyright remains with the ship's photography company.

This may only be one job but it's a step in the right direction and I'm really proud of myself for getting it, as they did go out to tender. Even if they did choose me because I was the cheapest, and Dave knows me, it's still an amazing feeling. It also makes it hard for me to hate *him*. Dave. He's a cheating, lying bastard and whenever I have a nice thought about him, I have to remind myself of that.

'Yeah, I think I'll be okay.' Jenna smiles, encouraging as ever. Our relationship has really blossomed over the last few months and it's almost like old times. There's just one thing that is between us now, the elephant in every room. Dave.

'So is his highness coming with us or will he be going to the event separately?' As we're staying in the town overnight the company has sprung for hotel rooms. Jenna is staying in with me so she can help with the photography equipment, yet I can't help but think there's more to it than that. The event starts at 3pm but we called ahead and have checked in early so we can get our stuff together and be at the zoo for 2pm.

Jenna rolls her eyes; she has remained tight-lipped about Dave and the events of that evening. I'm not even sure if they're breaking up or staying together. I don't think she has discussed what we witnessed with him and she has avoided any social interactions where they would go as a couple like the plague.

'He'll go in with his work friends, I think. Seems tidier,' Jenna says dismissively, clearly trying to get off the subject of Dave, but I'm not letting her get away with it that easily.

'Um, okay. So what's going on with you two?' I tentatively ask, searching for any clues.

I have asked several times and been treated to a myriad of reactions from being told to mind my own business to her silently leaving the room. I think about letting it go but I hate the idea of my sister remaining in an unhappy marriage, letting him cheat on her. She's worth so much more than that. I'm trying to remain supportive. Perhaps right now, on such an important day I shouldn't bring it up, but I can't help myself. I need to know. Will he be my ex-brother-in-law soon? Will I have to stop pretending everything is okay between us? On the few occasions I've seen Dave it's been excruciatingly awkward. I've found it difficult to meet his gaze and when he tries to joke with me like he normally does, I can't find anything he says in the slightest bit funny, so it falls flat.

Jenna sighs and sits down on one of the double beds. 'I know this is frustrating for you. I hope you can

137

understand my position, he is my husband. I love him and I'm trying to make it work.'

This is the most she has ever given me. I latch onto it like a leach, eager to know more.

'What did the bastard say when you confronted him? How long has it been going on? Is it over?' I want to run off every question that has popped into my mind over the last few months since that awful night, but I stop myself as I sense Jenna withdrawing into herself again. I've idly wondered whether attractive blonde will be at the do, but I daren't ask. Jenna must be thinking it too.

She bows her head and mumbles something quietly. I'm almost too scared to ask her to repeat it but I need to know so I go ahead.

'I didn't confront him, okay? Let's drop it now. I don't want to talk about it anymore.' And just like that she closes up tight as a clam. Will that be it now? Will we never speak of it again? At least I know now. I wish I hadn't been there that night if she was never going to do anything about it. I'll never be able to be normal around him. It would have been better if we hadn't stalked him.

I imagine her continuing her everyday routine ironing his shirts, cooking his dinner, chatting to him about his day like her world hasn't collapsed. I feel incredibly sad for her. I don't say anything more, what is there to say? I go over and give her a hug, it's not long before she pulls away and I know I don't need to say anymore, I'm always here for her if she needs me.

Sisters.

A few hours later and the event has been a roaring

success. I'm going to have lots of photographs to work with from the candid shots with the animals, the group photos and the hilarious snaps of the outdoor games. It's been a really good laugh and I've thoroughly enjoyed myself. There was the usual giant Jenga and tic-tac-toe but they also had a huge ring where staff dressed up in inflatable sumo suits and fought each other. It was hard to keep my camera steady because I was giggling so much. I've had some compliments and a few people even asked for my card. I'm feeling elated with how it's all gone. Jenna has been amazing and I can't wait to see her pictures. She's following my directions perfectly which is making the event as stress free as possible. She's everything you could want in an assistant. I note to myself that I must ask her to help out again for other events, assuming her snaps are good enough and I get more work.

It's into the evening now and I'm photographing portraits of people with their partners and work colleagues. Jenna is expertly queuing everyone up and giving them information about how to view the photographs afterwards. I've kept an eye out over the evening but I've not seen a sign of attractive blonde. I couldn't decide whether seeing her would be good or bad, did I want to see her so I could convince myself she was just a colleague? Although how would that explain why were they dining alone?

Dave interrupts my thoughts. 'I need a picture of me and my darling wife,' he says grabbing Jenna's arm and pulling her into him. 'I feel like I've hardly seen you all evening.' He hugs her close. 'You're keeping her very busy.' Dave looks pointedly at me, trying for a cheeky grin but it goes down like a lead balloon.

'Okay, get together.' I force a smile and try not to

treat him any differently from everyone else I've photographed, but I find it hard to control my tone. I've tried to keep my interactions with him to a minimum since the night we stalked him. It's such a shame because we used to have such a good friendship. He was good to my sister, my nephew and niece, and I liked him but now I feel like I don't know him at all. How must Jenna feel? If he can't be trusted, surely no man can.

Men? Are they all the same? Unreliable? I'm doing well on my list but the only item remaining is dating and I think I will keep that one on there a little longer. Denise keeps mentioning a potential date, but I'm not ready. There's no rush, especially when the world is filled with cheats, liars and losers.

Click, click. 'This is great isn't it, honey? It'll be nice to have a new photo of us around the house.' I try not to look at Jenna as the whole encounter is making me uncomfortable, he's laying it on thick. Perhaps he thinks she may have worked it out. When men cheat don't they act super nice to their spouses because of the guilt? Is that a thing? Getting them extra flowers and gifts for no reason.

'Hmm, yes.' Jenna smiles along but I can see that the smile doesn't really reach her eyes. If I'm finding it hard to control my feelings she must be too and I wonder how long she can go on like this, living a lie.

'Is everything okay?' he asks, concern filling his eyes. I really had no idea what a wonderful actor my brother-in-law is.

'Yes, fine just tired. Been a long night,' Jenna reassures him. She gestures to me and the queue behind them. 'Better be getting on.'

♥♥♥

I'm packing away the equipment when Dave comes over. I'm pleased to say I've not seen attractive blonde all night but it doesn't make it any less awkward between us.

'Do you know if something is up with Jenna? Have I done something?' he asks, searching my face.

I'm thrown, I'm not sure how to respond. He knows bloody well what he's done but as she hasn't told him she knows; he thinks he's getting away with it. God, I wish I could say what I really think of him but instead I respond blandly.

'No, she's fine, just tired like she said.' I keep my voice even and flat. Gone are the days of our camaraderie, no banter here.

'Okay.' He searches my face. 'Are you sure?' He really does look concerned and I think back to how I would have reacted to him before all of this but I can't bring myself to offer him any kindness. I'll protect my sister; I won't say anything about it to him but it doesn't mean I will forget.

'Quite sure, I'm knackered too,' I say concentrating on the light boxes, hoping he'll catch a hint.

'Okay, well I think it all went really well with the photos.' He smiles warmly trying to engage me in conversation.

'Oh, um yes, better get on.' I turn back to the lights and start to take the soft boxes off. Even if he did get me this job that doesn't make everything okay.

'Need a hand?' he asks.

'No, you go and enjoy the party. It'd take me longer to explain how it all goes. Easier if I do it myself,' I say through gritted teeth. I'm finding it harder and harder to hold my tongue and I hate speaking to him now.

'If you're sure.' He starts to walk away then I see him hesitate and look back at me with a puzzled look on his face.

Fucking cheating bastard.

Chapter 18

I'm awoken by a loud ringing noise and I turn over in bed trying to find the source, my eyes slowly beginning to adjust to the darkness. What is the time and why is someone calling me? I may go to bed earlier than others but this feels late. To be fair it could be 10.30pm or 5am for all I know.

'Hello,' I croak, trying to focus my mind.

'Oh, sorry did I wake you? Were you already asleep?' Jenna asks softly.

I look at my phone to see that it's 1am, of course she bloody woke me. Why is Jenna calling me at this ungodly hour?

'Yes, it's 1am, what else would I be doing?' I say flatly trying to shake myself awake. 'What's up?' I say more brightly; I have a feeling I know what's coming.

'I'm sorry. I wasn't going to call,' she hesitates, 'But I needed to speak to someone. I need to know. I need to find out. It's been driving me crazy since Dave's works do. I found myself looking at everyone wondering if they knew. If I was a complete mug. I felt embarrassed, Alma. I've known a lot of those people for years and I kept wondering if they were pitying me behind my back? Or even worse, laughing at me? I can't bear it anymore.' It all rushes out of Jenna in one long stream, all the thoughts that have clearly been running through her mind since the stalking night. I bet she's not even been to sleep yet.

This has been a long time coming and I have been waiting for it, though it's taken longer than I anticipated. Although it would have been better if it hadn't come in the middle of the night. Truthfully, I'd expected her to ask him straight away. It doesn't seem like the Jenna I knew as a child, all action first and think later but I can see she's a lot more sensitive and secretive than I gave her credit for. We are quite alike really.

'I've done some snooping and I've found out her name. Roma. He had it written in his work diary that day. It has to be her.' She talks in hushed tones and I imagine Dave and the children asleep upstairs oblivious to what's going on. Why didn't she just wake him up and ask him?

'Okay, what is it you want to do? Why don't you just speak to him? Is he not there now?' I ask hoping that I can go back to sleep, I bet it'll take me ages to drop off now though. I involuntarily roll my eyes, relieved that Jenna cannot see me.

Jenna avoids the question. 'He has another dinner with Roma next week,' she blurts. I'm not sure what she's thinking when she tells me this.

'Do you want to go along to the dinner? I didn't think you wanted to cause a scene in a restaurant. You made us leave last time,' I remind her of our last stakeout, I don't really fancy a repeat. It took a while for things to get back to normal between us after that.

'Hmm, maybe. Perhaps. I was thinking we may need your camera,' she says slowly emphasizing the camera part to make her plan clear.

I'm wide-awake now, this next stakeout sounds like it's going up a notch.

'Okay, well can we speak about this tomorrow maybe?' I ask.

'Oh yes, sorry. Want to come over to mine after work? Dave is working late.' I can hear the sigh in her voice as she says this.

'Yes, see you then. Bye.' I switch off my phone and lie flat on my back staring up at the ceiling. Now we're doing stakeouts with a camera, maybe I've missed my calling and I should have been a private investigator; I chuckle to myself. I toss and turn trying to get back to sleep, eventually falling into a deep slumber.

'So what's the plan?' I ask as we sit together in Jenna and Dave's living room.

'We're going to follow them and take pictures of them together so I can confront him properly. I need my evidence and then if needs be, I can get a divorce.' She reveals this while watching my face carefully for any reaction.

Wow, we're at divorce already. I'm shocked she hasn't even had the conversation with him but is already thinking divorce. I'm not really sure how to respond. I've been through break ups and the one with Nick put me through the wringer, but a divorce?

Jenna and Dave have been married for sixteen years. I think back to their beautiful, simple wedding, just family. There were only twenty of us and I was the youngest one there, just eleven years old. Jenna was twenty-one. Mum and Dad had thought she was too young, still finishing her degree. What was the rush they asked? Dave and Jenna were determined, they were in love. It seemed so romantic to me at the time, swirling around in my pink bridesmaid dress. I thought they'd be together forever.

'Okaaayyyy. Well let's wait and see what happens when you *actually* talk to him before you jump to divorce.' Perhaps there's still hope for them.

'He's just another cheating bastard and I'm not standing for it. You've inspired me.' I can see Jenna physically rise up in her seat. Good for her, she shouldn't stand for it. No one should stand for the pricks, cheaters or losers.

'When are you going to confront him? Do you need the photos immediately?'

'I've arranged sleepovers for the kids that night,' she explains. 'I'm going to do it when he gets back from dinner. Then I'm going to kick him out. He can find somewhere else for the night.' I'm taken aback by how much she has thought this through, but I suppose it's been a long time coming. 'I'll ring and let you know when he's gone,' she adds ruefully.

'Of course. You know I'm here for you.' I can't believe she has said she needs me; our relationship is so much stronger now. One good thing has come out of all this heartache, we have each other and our bond is stronger than ever. We don't need men. But I hope it doesn't end in divorce for Jenna and Dave.

A week later, it's 6.55pm and we're waiting in Jenna's

car outside the restaurant. Roma the beautiful blonde is already in situ – she's keen – and sat at the same table in the window where we can see and photograph them clearly.

Like clockwork Dave arrives at 7.00pm and strolls into the restaurant. There's the same show of kisses and cuddles and I get some good shots of this. These will definitely be good for Jenna if she does want a divorce. Roma is a knockout in a full-length green dress, with beautiful beading and embroidery, I bet it cost a bomb. It's a lovely restaurant but the dress seems over the top to me.

'So how long do you want to stay for?' I ask, breaking the silence. I've already snapped loads of photos of them greeting, I'm not really sure what more we need; they're hardly going to have sex in the middle of the restaurant.

'Hmm, I don't know, maybe a bit longer? What are the photos like?'

'Yes, I got the greeting, I don't know what else they may do. Want to stay until they leave?' I check, hoping that we won't have to sit here through the whole meal but I'm remaining supportive if that's what Jenna really wants to do.

'I don't think so. I don't need to see the whole show. Let's just sit a little longer. Tell me how your photography is going? Any interest from the works do?' Jenna smiles and turns towards me, taking her eyes off Dave and Roma for the first time since he entered the restaurant.

I smile. 'Actually, it's been pretty good. I've had a request for a family shoot. They thought the ones I took of your kids were fab, very natural. I've also got a wedding, it's only small but they had someone let them down. It's in a few months. Thinking of that, I was wondering if you would like to come along with me?' I ask, praying she'll say yes, Jenna was a godsend at the works do. Her people management and organisational skills could certainly come in useful during the hustle and bustle of a wedding.

'Really? As your assistant?' Jenna looks pleased and shocked, it's lovely to see something other than sadness on her face.

'Yes, some of the shots you took at the do were really good. It'd be great if you could do some candid pictures at the wedding. Also, you can help me with set up.' Also, if she's going to be without Dave, she will need an income of her own, I think sadly.

Jenna looks chuffed. I'm so pleased I asked her because she really did do a good job. I know having her there with me will make the day even more enjoyable. I'm looking forward to doing this together, we could be a photography team.

Jenna smiles to herself and then looks over at Dave again. Her expression drops and I can see the clouds of sadness creeping back in.

'Let's go, I think we've got enough,' she says, pulling the car away swiftly.

It's 11pm and I'm waiting by the phone for the call from Jenna. I know she was planning to confront him as soon as he came in but how late would he be? Surely he'd be back by now. But if the conversation goes on for some time, and let's face it, it will, then perhaps I need to give it a bit longer. By 12.30am I've called Jenna three times without response. I'm starting to get worried now. She'd have called if she needed me, I tell myself. I decide to go to bed, but I'll be round at Jenna's first thing in the morning. I leave my phone on loud just in case.

I sleep in late and wake up to find no messages from Jenna. Puzzled and worried, I pull on yesterday's clothes and go straight to Jenna's house to check she's okay.

I bang loudly on the door several times before there's any answer. A lot of shuffling and rattling of keys against the door ensues and then Dave pulls the door open slightly and peers out at me.

Dave? What the actual fuck is he doing here?

Well now I know she's confronted him I see no need for niceties anymore. It feels good to stop pretending and give way to how I really feel.

'Where's Jenna?' I ask trying to peer past him with a look of distain on my face. I can barely stand the sight of him.

He starts to answer but I have no interest in hearing what this cheating weasel has to say so I push the door open and stomp roughly past him and call for Jenna.

'Ouch,' yelps Dave. 'What's up with you?' The cheek of him.

'You bloody well know what's up with me, you cheating bastard.' I start to really let it go now. 'Where's Jenna? You didn't make *her* leave, did you? What an absolute arsehole. Where is she?'

Dave looks startled, did Jenna not have the conversation with him last night? And where the fuck is she?

As Dave is about to answer I see Jenna appear at the top of the stairs wrapped in a big towel with her hair piled on top of her head in a turban.

'Jen,' Dave calls up to her, 'I think you need to come down here and talk to your sister. She keeps calling me a cheating bastard.'

'You are,' I hiss at him.

Jenna disappears for a moment and reappears in her dressing gown. She hurries downstairs and ushers me into the living room while Dave looks between us.

'I'll make coffee,' he says, going out to the kitchen; I hear him filling the kettle. I can't believe he's not left. Why's he still even here? Never mind making coffee.

'What's going on? Why is that bastard still here? Why didn't you call me last night?' I rush to get my questions out. I've not even given her a chance to get dressed but I need to know what's going on right now.

'Oh, sorry, by the time we stopped talking it was really late and I didn't want to wake you up,' she says, looking guilty.

'So?' I ask, waiting for the explanation as to why he's still here. 'Have you just forgiven him after all that?' I can't believe it, I'm so disappointed in her.

Jenna looks down at her hands and mumbles. 'He wasn't cheating.' Her face reddens. 'She was a client.'

'What?' I say. 'Why the big displays of affection then and the dressing up, looked a lot like a date to me.'

'Yeah, her husband was there too. We couldn't see him from where we were, the angle was wrong. *His* name is Roma and so is his company. The beautiful blonde is his wife. They're Italian, very friendly and kissy, and she was dressed for *him*. Her husband. They were going out dancing after dinner.'

I look at Jenna, I can't believe it, this is ridiculous. He's explained it away and she's just accepted it.

'Oh, all sounds very convenient,' I say, rolling my eyes. I can't believe how gullible she is. 'And you believe all that crap?'

'He's telling the truth; I know he is because I know him.'

'You said he was cheating on you and you knew he was because you *know* him.' I spit the words at her, just in case she's forgotten them.

Jenna sighs. 'He also showed me emails from Roma and this…' She holds up her phone where she has pulled up a website called *Roma* and has pressed on the homepage. There's a picture of the beautiful blonde with an older handsome man: Roma. 'He was there too that night. Dave said we can even talk to Roma if needs be, but I trust him now. We chatted into the early hours of the morning and it felt so good for us both to reconnect,' she says, her face colouring. 'He's promised to try and work less so he can be at home more with me and the kids, especially now his promotion has gone through. The pressure has eased and he has just landed a huge client. Roma.'

I watch Jenna's face. She believes Dave. Why shouldn't I? But I don't know what to say. I'm speechless. I'm happy for her but I find myself feeling insanely jealous. When will I find my happy ever after? I feel like I'm going to lose my sister all over again. I can feel tears prickle at my eyes, of course this is what I want for her but a little selfish part of me is sad we aren't in this together, just the two of us. It's just the two of *them*.

Dave edges into the room with a tray of coffee and biscuits.

'Am I okay to be in here now?' he asks looking between me and Jenna and slowly settling the tray on the coffee table.

I flush with embarrassment thinking about how I've

treated him over the past few months. Although it was all Jenna's fault.

'Umm, yes, I think I owe you a bit of an apology,' I start sheepishly. I hope he doesn't make this any harder than it has to be.

His eyes twinkle. 'I must admit it wasn't my favourite thing being called a cheating bastard. I'll forgive you though, I know you were just being a good sister.' He gives me a smile and I'm relieved that things might not be awkward between us. 'I knew something was up at the works do but I just couldn't work out what it was. Figured you may have been nervous getting into your photography again or something.' He shrugs.

'I'm glad it's all come out now and been resolved,' I say hoping that we can draw a line under this and go back to our relationship being like it was before. I feel stupid and embarrassed.

'I know, I feel so silly,' Jenna says self-consciously. 'I should have just asked you.' She cuddles up to Dave who puts his arm around her and pulls her closer.

'Did you guys really do a stakeout dressed in black and wearing wigs?' He starts to laugh. 'I can't believe I didn't spot you. Next time you're on one of your famous stakeouts can I come too?' He smirks. 'Perhaps you girls missed your calling as detectives, although actually you jumped to all the wrong conclusions, so perhaps you didn't.' He's really belly-laughing now and it's infectious. Jenna and I start to laugh too. It feels good to let go of all my bad feelings towards Dave. I'm relieved for my niece and nephew as well.

So perhaps *all* men aren't cheats.

Jenna could have messaged me though, and saved me the embarrassment of coming around here all guns blazing.

Chapter 19

'Hey, hey come in, come in.' Helen, the blushing bride, ushers me into the house and leads me through to the conservatory. It's all modern and airy, like the rest of the house. Everything is cream, the walls, the carpets, the furniture. It's very organised and tidy, nowhere near as cluttered as I'm used to but I can't help feel it lacks a bit of character.

'The videographer should be here soon. I guess you guys will end up working closely today,' Helen says, chuckling to herself. 'He's a friend of mine so, he's doing me a *massive* favour. Do you need a drink or anything before you get started?'

I start to put my kit together. 'No, no I'm fine, just tell me where your dress, shoes and accessories are and remind me when you're having your hair and make-up done and I'll get started.' I smile broadly, I've been looking forward to this day for weeks and now it's finally here. I'd be lying if I said I wasn't nervous. I hardly slept a wink last night thinking about all the shots I want to take and then all the ways it could go wrong, the disaster scenarios.

'Upstairs in my room, first left on the landing. Hair at 8am and make-up at 9.30am,' she instructs.

Everything is very organised here; I imagine the groom won't even get out of bed until the bride's make-up is being applied. It'll be a very different morning for the groom. He won't have the flurry of people around him, perhaps a best man or his parents but nothing like this. His preparation will consist of a shower, shave and putting on a nice suit, maybe some extra special aftershave.

Helen and Karl are getting married at noon but I know the lead up and preparation takes hours so I've arrived at 7.30am sharp to be able to get everything photographed. I bet Helen and the girls have been up since 6am or earlier. This part of the morning is usually more relaxed, depending on the bride; Helen is practically lying down she's so chilled. I'm excited to be photographing someone who doesn't sweat the small stuff. Bridezilla she certainly is not. If something goes wrong today I think she'd probably just laugh it off. For someone I've only just met I really like her and I'm thrilled to spend her special day with her.

It's a small wedding, only twenty in the day, but she has an unusually large bridal party; she's one of five sisters. Helen is Irish so the house is loud and buzzing with Irish accents and excitement. I go upstairs into Helen's room and take photos of her dress and her bridesmaid dresses in all their different configurations. I arrange her wedding dress so it is flowing down the mirror to show it off to its full affect. I also take shots of her bridal jewellery and her shoes and then go downstairs to see what the girls are up to. They all have those dressing gowns on saying what their roles are in the wedding: bride, bridesmaid, maid of honour. I take an array of photos with them posing, plus some natural candid photos while they get ready. The bland and tidy house is starting to get messed up. I search Helen's face for any signs of stress but she's so swept up in it all that I don't think she's even noticed the mess.

I'm really enjoying myself, experimenting with angles and light. I can't help but think that these are going to look great on my website, when I finally get it up and running but they'll still look great on my Facebook page for now. It certainly helps that Helen and Karl are a very attractive couple, making them look amazing will not be a difficult feat.

Jenna will be taking photographs of Karl and his best man. I've written her strict instructions and she is to message me if she has any worries. I've gone over in detail what she needs to do. Jenna said it was overkill but I'm just covering my bases and making sure she knows what is expected. It'll only probably take her around half an hour to do their shots. Then she's getting a lift over with the groom and will take some photos in the church. If she's as helpful as she was at Dave's work do then I'll definitely be employing her for future weddings. It's good to have a second photographer.

A few hours later and Helen is having her make-up done. Her hair is finished and looks stunning in a soft up-do with curly tendrils. The doorbell goes as I'm going through my bag in the porch and I jump and almost drop my camera. That was disaster scenario number one from last night's worrying – dropping my camera. Thank God it didn't actually happen.

'I'll get it,' I call out to prevent a stampede of Irish women come running down the stairs meaning I might almost drop my camera again.

155

'Okay, it's probably the videographer,' Helen shouts back in a singsong voice. She certainly is feeling upbeat this morning. Who could blame her? The champagne she's been sipping is probably helping too.

I turn and pull open the door and freeze when I see the person standing on the porch, video camera in hand, natty backpack on too. My mouth hangs open like a goldfish.

Oh. My. God.

I can honestly say I wasn't expecting to see *him* again. His face turns from surprise to anger before he manages to compose himself and show a neutral expression. I don't think this disaster scenario popped up last night. This would have been top of my list.

'What are you doing here?' I blurt out, not able to hide my distain.

'What do you think?' he says, waving his video camera and looking beyond me. 'Are you going to let me in then?' His voice is gruff as he attempts to push past me before I pull myself together and step aside.

I'm shocked, I thought Helen was such a nice girl, why is she friends with him?

Lewis the Loo Loser.

I follow him upstairs to see Helen who jumps up and makes a big show of hugging him and introducing him to a couple of her sisters.

'Have you guys been introduced? Alma this is Lewis, Lewis this is Alma.' She smiles patting him on the back. 'We work together and Lewis is doing me a huge favour, thanks Lewis. You've saved me a bomb.'

I can feel the heat rise up my face, undoubtedly colouring it red. I don't know what to say. Yes, Helen we have met, we went on what I thought was a good date until I went to the toilet and Lewis promptly left. I don't feel like this is good wedding talk. I stand there mouth dropping and wondering what he's going to say. Is he going to humiliate me? Will he say I was such a bad kisser he just had to leave? I still can't believe he is here. I need to shake this off and compose myself.

'Yes, nice to meet you,' Lewis says briefly, glancing my way then making a point of busying himself pressing all the buttons on his video camera. Does he even know how to work that thing?

'Um, you too.' Could this be any more awkward? Does he not even remember me? I could have sworn he looked annoyed at the door. I didn't disappear on *him* when he went to the loo so what does he have to be pissed off about? Then I picture it, the ice cream running down his face and the stinky sock flying through the air on a perfect collision course with his head. Such a sweet moment. That makes me smile briefly and I make my excuses and escape to the loo so I can try and compose myself before spending the day with Lewis the Loo Loser.

Safely locked in the loo I send Jenna a warning text.

Alma: Lewis the Loo Loser is here.

Jenna: What? The guy who left you at the pub?

Alma: Yeah, he's the fucking videographer today. He's going to spend the whole day under my feet. Everyone is acting like he's this really lovely, amazing guy.

Jenna: What a wanker. Have you said anything to him?

Alma: No and I'm not going to and neither are you. We're professionals and we are going to just concentrate on the job. I was just warning you so when you see him you don't go crazy. I'm not even sure he knows who I am.

Jenna: How many people has he abandoned in the toilets? Of course he knows who you are.

Alma: How should I know? Perhaps he does it every week.

Jenna: Alright, alright. Sorry. We'll do an amazing job and show that prick.

Alma: Thanks Jenna. I'll see you at the church.

The irony that I'm in the loo is not lost on me when I'm thinking about Lewis. I hope he does his disappearing act by the time I come back out.

No such luck. He's still here and is lording it around the place making the Irish ladies laugh. A few of them have mentioned how handsome he is and what a nice guy he is to me like they're trying to set me up. Little do they know what a secret arse he really is. I won't tell them; this is neither the time nor the place and I know I need to maintain a professional air. This is my first proper job after all and I'll be damned if I'm letting *him* ruin it. Helen said he was a friend doing her a favour, so surely I won't see him again on the wedding circuits.

I just have to get through the rest of today then I'll never have to see him again.

Chapter 20

I've managed to keep a reasonable distance from Lewis at the house and because I arrived so early he went off to shoot the dress and accessories which gave me a much-needed break from seeing his wanker face. Every time I feel annoyed, I just imagine the ice cream dripping down him and of course the stinking sock; it makes me feel so much better.

'You don't mind taking Lewis in your car, do you? He's had some car trouble and got a taxi over this morning but surely you have a little space in your car? Sorry to ask. Would you mind? Our cars are packed.' Helen flutters her eyelashes; Karl doesn't stand a chance when Helen really wants her way. A strong Irish woman indeed and who am I to say no on her wedding day? It would make me seem petty and mean.

'Yeah, of course that's fine.' I grit my teeth and smile. Oh joy, now I get to be in a confined space with *him*. I hope he doesn't think this means I want to make small talk. Or that I've forgiven him for what he did to me.

'I'll go tell him. He'd have never asked you himself

and would have got taxis all day.' She rolls her eyes. 'But there's really no need, is there? Thank you, you're a star. I really appreciate it.' She leans in and gives me a hug. 'He'll be so pleased,' she adds. If only she knew.

I hope against hope that the loo loser insists on going in a taxi but I know that Helen will convince him otherwise. She's seen a problem and found the perfect solution. A few of her sisters smiled and gave me a knowing look when Helen asked, one even winked. If only they really knew what Lewis is really like. How he really treats people. They wouldn't think he was so lovely then.

Lewis comes into the room having seemingly been strong-armed into agreeing. Great. This won't be awkward at all.

We finish up taking photos and videos of the girls all together and a final shot of Helen and her dad in the car before they head off to the venue.

We both climb into my Kia Picanto without saying a word. As I start the car up it dawns on me that I'm then going to have to drive him to the pub we're heading onto afterwards and perhaps home? Oh, what have I agreed to? Surely I'll be able to get out of driving him home. Also, I'll have Jenna with me so that should hopefully make it less awkward. Or more awkward?

'Um, thank you for the lift,' he says, after a few minutes of awkward silence I can feel his eyes on me. Perhaps he does know who I am and thinks it was me who launched the ice cream at him.

'That's fine,' I reply curtly, and stick the radio on and turn it up as high as I can stand to signal that we do not need to talk.

As we pull up to the venue, he jumps out and starts to unload his equipment at super speed. I grab my camera bags and head into the church to meet with Jenna and we choose our spot to photograph the ceremony. My shadow is hot on my heels and I'm beginning to feel even more irritated by him. If the video was not for Helen and Karl, I might be tempted to stand in front of his camera the whole day, but of course, I won't.

I take a few snaps of the nervous groom. Waiting and wondering if she'll definitely come, Karl looks like he could pass out. Perhaps his morning *hasn't* been so relaxed. I see Lewis step forward and shake Karl's hand before setting his equipment in place.

'Is that him? Wow he *is* hot,' Jenna whispers, staring straight at Lewis.

I cast her a look that says *shut the fuck up*. 'What? You've seen him before.' I don't know why she needed to say that.

'Well, just saying he looks hot in a suit and without ice cream all over his face.' She grins and I can't help but grin too at the memory.

'You go and see if there's any sign of Helen,' I tell Jenna.

Jenna disappears but is soon back and beckoning me from the door. I dash out to photograph Helen's arrival and, annoyingly, Lewis grabs his video camera and follows closely behind me.

Helen arrives in a flurry of activity; all the bridesmaids are buzzing around her, and I get swept back into the reason I'm here. I brush off my dank mood and get back into the zone, enjoying the summer sun and the perfect blue sky with just a few fluffy clouds to give it some atmosphere. The girls are giggly and bright in their magenta pink dresses and they look beautiful as they approach. I can see the proud expression on Helen's father's face and I relish capturing his awe and wonder. It's such a special time and I love that I'm seeing these moments. Moments that everyone doesn't get to see.

'We need to get back into position before Helen walks up the aisle,' I say rushing back into the church but Lewis has beaten me to it. How? Damn him, he now has two video cameras set up in the best positions. I can work around them easily but it's a pain as it means I'm constantly sweeping past him. I do my utmost to ensure we don't touch. I'd put Jenna here but as she's not as experienced as me, I can't take the risk because I need to make sure that these shots are perfect. The ceremony shots can be some of the most special moments you can get, a range of tears and laughter and then of course the elusive first kiss which *must* be captured.

'Would you mind moving over to the right? You're going to ruin my shot,' Lewis whispers gruffly. Who the fuck is he to be annoyed with me? I mean, I know he had some ice cream thrown at him but it was the least he deserved considering that he left me alone and humiliated in a pub. I'm trying my best to be composed but he's really starting to piss me off.

'Whatever,' I hiss, stepping aside. I have no interest in keeping up the nice pretence when Helen and Karl are not witnessing it and the more I look at him, the angrier I feel about it all.

He's getting a good range of shots and angles and if he wasn't such a wanker, I'd think he was a fairly good videographer. I get some beautiful photographs during the ceremony and of the moment Helen enters and Karl looks astonished, so pleased she picked him. His eyes are filled with tears; it really is beautiful.

There's a funny moment where he tries to put the wedding ring on the wrong finger while she tries to subtly indicate it's the wrong finger and guide him to the right one, but everyone can see what is happening.

Eventually she stage-whispers, 'No, that one.' Everyone laughs and I can see Karl visibly relax, the ice has been broken.

I bet that moment will be watched again and again on the video. I'm enjoying every second of this, even the loo loser can't ruin this for me. At the end of the ceremony I get the perfect shot of the first kiss. They're going to love these photos; I can't wait to show them.

I've booked the next few days off work because I'm just so eager to be able to go over all of the photos and start editing. I want to stay in my photography bubble for a few more days before I have to return to my mundane job. I now know this is what I should be doing. I feel stupid for giving it all up for a man. This is my calling and I should never have let Nick the Prick take my passion away, but it's back now. I won't let it go again. I hope I can turn this into a career.

Over the next hour I take an array of group shots and some of the happy couple by the church. Every time I look around, Lewis is by my side getting video of everything and I try my best to ignore him. God, he's annoying. Finally, it's time to move onto their local pub where they've booked a private room for them and their twenty guests. Jenna, Lewis and I climb into my increasingly packed car. I'm just glad this time he doesn't have to sit in the front.

The pub is a twenty-minute journey; as I start to drive I go over everything with Jenna checking that she's got all the images we need. We have a list of photographs that they were particularly keen to get. In the rear view mirror I can see Lewis's smirking face, he's really starting to wind me up but I bite my tongue. Now is not the time or place.

I am also going to take them away for a little couple alone shoot after the meal and Jenna is going to stay at the pub to take photographs of the guests. Lewis has remained silent. Hurray for small mercies, but he suddenly pipes up.

'Could I come along to that?' he mutters, his smirk has disappeared and he sounds almost embarrassed to ask. Good. I'm not going to make this easy for him.

'Come along to what?' I ask, feigning ignorance. He's going to need to ask me properly.

'The couple alone shoot. I'd like to capture some of those moments. They'd look good on the video.'

What can I say? I don't want him there, most definitely not, but I don't think I have any choice.

'Yes. Fine,' I say. I know Helen will just convince me anyway, what's the point in saying no when it's not really my choice.

It's like the sound of Lewis's voice has reminded Jenna that he is there. She turns to him after giving me a mischievous look.

'What's the name of the pub that we're going to again?'

'Kerby's' I answer before he does. I don't know why she's asking this; she knows perfectly well which pub we're going to. It was listed on my extensive notes in case, for some reason, we had to travel to the pub separately; disaster scenario number four.

'Oh, I thought it was the Moon bar,' she says and I feel my face colour at the mention of that bar and the night he abandoned me. What the hell is she playing at? What's she trying to do? 'Have you ever been to that one Lewis?' she asks, sounding innocent.

I narrow my eyes at Jenna and she gives a little shrug. Why the hell is she bringing this up now? I contemplate turning the radio on again but curiosity has got the better of me.

I glance in the mirror at Lewis; he has the good grace to at least looks a bit embarrassed. Thank God we're pulling into the pub now.

'Why am I thinking of that pub?' Jenna muses making a show of stroking her chin. She's such a terrible actor.

'I don't know but I really think you should drop it,' I mutter. I'll find a space and in just two minutes we'll be out of this car and this hell will be over.

'No, I remember now. It's where Lewis waited till you went to the toilets and then abandoned you on a date, without a word, not even a text. That's a pretty shitty thing to do. Isn't it?'

That's it the cat's out of the bag. I'm mortified but really it should be him who is ashamed.

'Shut up,' I hiss at Jenna. I'm not pleased with her for doing this right now. I've rocketed into the first parking space I've found and am already jumping out of the car.

'Wait, what?' Lewis suddenly becomes more animated, leaning forward to check what he's just heard.

'I don't want to talk about this right now,' I say grabbing my bag and making a break for it. I wish the ground would swallow me up. I'm furious with Jenna. Why did she do that?

Now he knows I care about what he did to me.

Chapter 21

The rest of the wedding goes by without a hitch and thankfully, I manage to exchange hardly any words with Lewis. Much to my relief. Even when we're doing the couple alone shoot, I manage to maintain a reasonable distance. I'm still enjoying the day but it has definitely taken the edge off my buzz. I keep picturing myself wandering around the pub looking for Lewis and I feel irritated, annoyed and embarrassed when I remember people staring at me in the Moon bar that night. Why did he have to be here? I was doing just fine without him. Great even. I'm going to give Jenna a big telling off in the car, I'm so pissed off that she mentioned it. It's made me relive the whole sorry affair.

It's 7pm and the evening guests have begun to arrive. There's only around two hours of shooting left now as the first dance is at 8pm. We do our best to photograph as many of the guests as possible in groups and get some lovely natural shots as they talk. My feet are really getting sore now from all of the standing. I'd forgotten what a long day weddings are. I've loved it but I'm definitely beginning to lag. I'm just grabbing a well needed drink of water at the bar when I feel a hand on my arm.

'Can we talk?' It's Lewis. What now? I don't want to talk to him, I'm so angry with him, I just want this to be over and to go home.

'No. I don't want to talk to you.' He starts to protest but I cut him off. 'I don't care what you have to say. It wasn't a good date anyway. If you hadn't left, I would have. That kiss was terrible.'

That's completely not true but I'm trying to save face. With that I turn on my heels and run into the women's bathroom. He can't get me in here. Bringing up the kiss has reminded me of how amazing it really was. I almost want to cry; I hate to admit even to myself what a great date that was. Well, up until he left that is. The kiss was out of this world and I had wanted more. I rub my hands through my hair. I'm emotionally and mentally drained.

Just as I'm washing my hands I hear them announce the first dance. Shit. I run out of the bathroom and push my way through the crowds gathered around the dance floor to get my shots. I almost run into Lewis but I manage to avoid him at the last second, accidently kicking him in the leg as I go by.

'Okay, I get that you don't want to talk,' he says gruffly, pulling his leg away. What's got up his butt? What a wanker.

Over the next few days I shut myself in my room and go to town editing all of the images. Checking the crop, making sure that the exposure is just right, trying to salvage any shots which are good but my flash didn't go off and turning them to black and white.

There are a really good range and Jenna has done an amazing job too, I've had to go through and re-crop quite few of her photographs but for a novice she has potential and she has paid special attention to all of my lists and ensured she's got everything on it. She can definitely continue to be my assistant. If I wasn't still so pissed at her I would message her and tell her.

I have a viewing arranged for a week Monday so will have to see her then but for now she can stew in her juices. Of course I will forgive her, but not too easily. Lewis did kind of deserve to know he was a wanker even if it was humiliating for me.

'So we're all good now? I'm sorry about what I said to Lewis at the wedding.' Jenna gives me a cheeky grin. 'But he did deserve to know he was in the wrong.'

I've picked Jenna up and we're on our way over to Helen and Karl's to look at the photographs. I'm excited for the viewing, to show them the images, I really think they're going to love them.

'Hello, hello. Come in.' Helen ushers us in. 'There's quite a few of us for the viewing I hope you don't mind.'

'Oh um, of course not. But just remember they're your wedding photos and it's up to you what you want to do with them.' I exchange a look with Jenna screaming that this is not what I was expecting.

As we head into the living room there are three of her sisters huddled together on the sofa, her husband is sat on a chair and there are a couple of other chairs, two for us and presumably other guests who haven't yet arrived. The room is feeling pretty packed and it's making me feel nervous. I wasn't expecting this and I jot a note down to myself to be more specific about how a viewing works with my next wedding. You live and learn.

It's understandable that Helen would want to show everyone but I usually prefer the viewings just to be with the newly-weds. Otherwise other people's opinions can colour what they choose and I want to be sure they go away with exactly what *they* want. There are loads of delicious looking snacks laid out on the table. My mouth starts to water, I've not eaten all day because I've been preparing the last of the photographs and the slideshow.

'It'll take me a few minutes to get ready,' I say, connecting my laptop to their TV so we can view everything on the big screen. I signal to Jenna to give me a hand.

We'll watch all the images as a slideshow first, set to music. I've chosen their wedding song and a few songs that were popular at the wedding disco. I'm really proud of the photos and I hope they love them too.

'Ready to go,' I say. We're all set up and I'm anxious to get started.

'Could we just wait five minutes? We're still waiting on a few people.' Helen announces, indicating the empty seats.

As if they have been summoned there's a loud knock at the door. After some commotion and laughter in the hallway another sister tumbles into the room, followed by Lewis.

Oh great, my absolute favourite person. My stomach lurches and I suddenly stop feeling hungry. I really hope the images go down well now. Why does he always need to be here? Is Helen's sister his girlfriend? I subtly roll my eyes at Jenna who looks suitably horrified for me. I remind myself that after today I will never have to see him again. Although to be fair I thought *that* after the first, second and third time we met.

'Oh, I thought it was the video viewing,' he says, eyeing me and my plugged-in laptop suspiciously.

'Yes, yes, it is. I thought I said. We thought it'd be fun to do a bit of both, you know. Look at the photos and then watch the video?' Helen smiles and all her sisters join in, nodding and agreeing. We all know there's no point in arguing. Helen's going to get exactly what she wants. Karl, you poor sod, what have you married into? I look over at him sitting on the sofa, he has barely spoken two words to anyone since we arrived.

The wedding photos and the video go down really well. Everyone absolutely loves them but the evening doesn't go exactly to plan. I'd hoped they would be more decisive, choose their pictures and tell me how they want them, but between all the chatting and reminiscing about the wedding they haven't chosen even one. I'll have to come back and do it again.

I let Helen and Karl know this should be alone next time and make it really clear that means no video too. I'm not chancing seeing Lewis again. I tell them it's so they can take their time choosing an album or if they just want all the photos on a disc. I leave them with the price lists for everything. Upon Helen's insistence I stay to watch the video. It really is beautiful; it's also funny because we have used nearly all the same songs. Some of the ways he has filmed them have also given me some inspiration. It's good to look at other people's work. Even if they are losers.

'You two are really in sync,' one of the sisters giggles. 'Are you a duo? Video and camera, you totally should be.'

'Hmm.' I grimace and try and turn it into a laugh. We are not in sync and we are not a duo. 'No, we work independently. Only just met,' I say, giving Lewis a dirty look.

'Yeah you could be a double act though. You should think about it,' another sister agrees. I can feel my face blushing and I excuse myself to go to the bathroom to splash cold water on it.

As the evening comes to a close everyone begins to leave. They've all had a good look at our albums and I think there's a good chance that some of the guests will order some photos too, which will be good for my sales. I go and have a glass of water and chat to Helen and Karl while Jenna and Lewis pack up the cameras. I'm so pleased I don't have to see Lewis's annoying face for much longer.

'You know he's single don't you.' Oh my God not this again. Why are they all obsessed with setting me and Lewis up?

'Not my type,' I say deadpan, trying to put an end to it. I don't know why they're so determined to keep on about this.

'Oh, okay. Sorry. I just thought, I don't know… you two look cute together. I'm a sucker for a bit of romance. Don't mind me, I'm always trying to set people up.' Helen laughs and Karl nods along, rolling his eyes and smiling.

Realisation hits, oh my God. That's why he's here tonight. It all makes sense now. How appropriate that she should have both viewings on the same night. This was on purpose. I can't blame her. If we hadn't already had a disastrous date, I might have been interested but she doesn't know about that. It appears he hasn't told her either so perhaps he is a bit ashamed of himself. So he damn well should be.

'I'd better be getting on,' I say putting an end to the conversation. I go back into the living room to give Jenna a hand with the albums. As I enter the room, I see her chatting with Lewis. Why is she talking to the enemy? I narrow my eyes at her to indicate I am not impressed.

'Better get all packed up,' I say loudly enough that Jenna gets the message. She comes scurrying over.

'What were you and the loo loser talking about?' I question Jenna as we head home.

'You,' she says bluntly. 'He wants to explain. You know he seems like a decent kind of guy. I think you should talk to him.' Jenna has certainly changed her tune.

'So you have a quick five-minute chat with him and you're on his side. Do you not remember what he did to me? I don't think he deserves my time. He had his opportunity and he chose to scuttle off when I went to the loo. So no, I'm not prepared to give him another chance.'

I scowl at her. She can see I'm absolutely fuming and doesn't attempt to press the subject any further.

We sit silently for the rest of the journey.

And just like that Lewis the Loo Loser has ruined my night.

Again.

Chapter 22

'What else do you need to get?' I ask. We've been shopping now for over three hours and I've had enough. Jenna could shop till she drops but that is just not me. We're picking up some things for Claire's birthday and the list of items to get for her presents and party seem absolutely endless. I don't remember getting this many gifts when I turned fourteen.

'I just want a birthday cake now and we're done.' She sighs, bored by my whinging.

'Shall we go for lunch now then?' I ask, I'm desperate for this to come to an end. I've had enough of looking at trinkets, jewellery and nail varnish. How much could one teenager possibly need?

'No, let's finish up and then we can go for lunch. We can go straight home afterwards.' She smiles, she knows I'm fed up and there's no point in me even attempting to hide it.

'Okay.'

We turn down Wood Street and walk along the pubs and restaurants, I can smell the food and it makes my stomach audibly grumble. We're both staring into the windows watching the happy customers. I wish I was one of them. I'm just trying to decide what kind of food I would like to eat when Jenna interrupts my thoughts.

'On second thoughts, I'm starving. How about that one.' She points to a café. It wasn't really where I had imagined we'd go for lunch. I was thinking a pub or something which would have larger meals.

'Or that pub over there.' I point, hoping to get my own way. Although I'm so desperate for a break I'll leap at the chance of anywhere.

'No, I think this one will be really good. I've heard good things,' Jenna says and I don't have the energy to fight. Also, if she's heard good things, I'm sure I'll find something delicious. Although at this point anything would do really.

We go in, check the menu board then give our order to the teenage girl behind the counter. I order a panini and the coffee I need to wake myself up and Jenna orders a scone and a cup of tea. We take our drinks and find a table; I hope I don't have to wait too long for my food, I'm starving. I take a big sip of coffee; it tastes so good. Maybe this place wasn't a bad choice after all. Jenna starts to stuff her scone in as quickly as possible, clearly she is hungry as well.

I glance around the café at the other diners and that's when I notice him. He's sat over near the window so I'm not sure why I didn't see him sooner. I have a sinking feeling that this is why Jenna chose this place. Lewis, the loo loser, is here. I cannot seem to shake this man off at the moment. At least this time I don't need to speak to him.

I turn to look at Jenna and I can see that she has noticed I've seen him. She gives me a sheepish grin. She knows full well what she has done. I'm thoroughly unimpressed.

'Sorry.' Although the grin on her face says she's anything but. 'I still think you should hear him out and when I saw him in the window I couldn't resist. Seems like fate to me.'

Nooo. Jenna won't quit, so typical of her and now I'm stuck here waiting for my food so I can't even leave. As if he's been summoned, Lewis notices us and does a double take. He's just finishing up and I can see him hesitate as he decides whether to come over. I'm praying he just leaves and that will be the end of that but I can see by his expression that the option to come over is winning his internal debate. He strolls over to our table looking nervous and fiddling with his hands.

'Hey, it's you,' he says, seeming as surprised as me. 'This is crazy. Do you think we could have that chat?' He glances between me and Jenna, while switching from foot to foot. I almost want to laugh at the ridiculousness of it all.

What am I supposed to do now? I'm not having this conversation with Jenna sitting here. I gesture to Jenna. 'I'm having lunch with my sister,' I say flatly, hoping he'll catch the hint and end the conversation.

'Oh, don't worry about me,' she says, gulping down the last of her scone and wiping the crumbs from her top. 'I'm all finished now and your food isn't even here yet. I need to pop to the bakery anyway.' As quick as a flash she downs her tea and practically sprints out of the door. I hope that tea was scalding hot. I'm sure she'll at least get indigestion from eating so fast. Good. She deserves it.

Lewis sits down in Jenna's seat. It's the moment of truth now. Now I have to hear him out and I really don't want to. I contemplate going to the toilet, after all he left when I did that last time. I wonder how long I need to be in there before he'd leave again. I suppose it didn't work at the wedding and it won't work now. If we're going to keep bumping into each other I'm going to have to hear whatever silly excuse he has.

'Look, I'm sorry about our first date,' he starts, trying to look into my eyes.

'Hmmm.' I nod, holding my gaze downwards and concentrating on my coffee. I'm not going to make this easy for him. I wait for him to spout his excuses.

'I tried to call you and I tried to contact you on *meant2b* but you weren't on it any longer and I guess you blocked my number?'

'Well you left when I went to the toilet. You humiliated me and I didn't much feel like having a chat about it. Okay?' I rush this out, feeling humiliated all over again, feeling the anger start to rise in my chest.

'But that's the thing, I did leave a message for you. I didn't just run off. There was an emergency. Didn't he give it to you? I…'

'Of course…' I say cutting him off. 'Are you worried I'll tell your friends what you're like? Don't try to make excuses to make yourself look better. I'm not buying it. If you left a message with someone why wouldn't they have told me?'

'No, I did. I told the barman to let you know I'd been called out on an emergency and that I'd call you later and I was sorry to leave suddenly. I described you to him, green polka dot dress, long, dark brown hair, pretty.' He says the last word shyly, watching me. I'm almost impressed he remembers what I was wearing.

Oh, flattery will get you nowhere with me but as he describes me, I think back to that awful night. I remember being in the toilets before I came down and my night was ruined. I was so excited about that date, my first since Nick the Prick, Lewis was about to restore my faith in men. I came out of the cubicle and looked over and there was my doppelganger, the girl I told to leave the toilets first. Green polka dot dress, long, dark brown hair, pretty.

My panini arrives, but I can't take a bite now.

'I really don't understand, the barman promised he'd let you know.' He shakes his head and rubs his face with confusion. I look up at him for the first time, straight into his eyes and I can see that he is being honest. He actually did leave me a message only it wasn't me who received the message, it was my double.

'Doppelganger,' I mumble.

'What?' he asks, looking puzzled.

'There was a girl in the toilets who had the same dress on and similar hair. She must have got your message, not me.' I shrug. 'Still, it's a shitty thing to leave while I'm in the loo. Why couldn't you wait and let me know?'

'My niece was in a car accident and my sister was on the phone, she was in such a state. I could hardly get any sense out of her and you'd just left for the toilets. I gave the barman the message and left straight away. She was on the phone to me the whole way there otherwise I'd have called or messaged you and then when I arrived at the hospital there was no time to do anything.'

'Oh, um.' I don't really know what to say. So perhaps it *was* a good date for him too. I'd felt such a connection with him and I'd enjoyed our time together, I thought we'd at least get a second date. 'Is your niece okay?' His poor sister, a memory of him talking about how close they were coming to mind. How she relies on him and there's no father on the scene. It makes sense she'd call him.

'Yes, she's fine, hardly a scratch on her. My sister had just got herself into a right state. I think she was in shock.' He smiles, his eyes sparkling. Before I manage to say anything, he adds, 'Although, I suppose it doesn't really matter because you said it was a horrible date anyway.' He shrugs, but I can tell he's bothered, the sparkle has left his eyes.

'What would you say to the person who left you in the middle of a date?' I ask, 'I was just trying to save face.'

'You've got a point there. Was the ice cream and the sock really necessary though? Although they make a lot more sense now.' He grins and I can't help but laugh. 'Please don't tell me that was one of your socks?'

Oh God, the horror. 'No, it wasn't. It was my nephew's and I think it'd been festering in the car for a while.' I chuckle at the thought.

'Good, because it stunk.'

'I know.' I stifle a giggle. 'Why didn't you say anything at Helen's? You pretended not to even recognise me,' I ask, wondering what was going through his mind.

'I assumed you'd got the message from the barman but were still pissed off with me. I know better now but at the time I thought you were pretty heartless to be annoyed when I'd said I'd be in touch later, and it *was* a real emergency. The kiss was so amazing that I thought we had a connection and you felt it too. I thought you'd understand.' He looks down, fiddling with his hands, embarrassed. 'When you threw the ice cream and the stinking sock at me, it sealed the deal.' He laughs, recovering from his earlier vulnerability.

So he did think the kiss was good. I can feel the butterflies in my stomach begin to return. 'I thought you were a teacher not a videographer?' I question, changing the subject because I don't want to discuss my revenge any longer.

'I am. The wedding was a bit of a passion project mixed in with a favour. I'm an art teacher. I work with Helen.'

Oh yes, I remember her saying they worked together now.

'I like lots of different forms of expression but I do really enjoy video. This is my first wedding though.'

I'm really surprised. 'That's amazing. I thought the video was really good.'

'Yes, and I thought your photos were really good. Are you still working at the bank? Holborns, is it?'

I'm impressed he remembers; he was obviously really listening on our date. I wish it had ended differently. Who knows where we would be now if it had? Would we still be dating?

'Yes, I'm still there for the time being but I've set up my own wedding photography business. I do portraits too.' I smile. It feels good to talk about my work and I feel proud of myself for a change instead of changing the subject to avoid death via boredom.

'So, what do you think, could we have a second date?' He looks down shyly, fidgeting with his hands. He seems so unsure of himself but I like that he's taking the risk of asking me out again when I could so easily turn him down.

'Do you promise not to leave when I go to the loo this time?' I tease.

'Only if you promise not to order ice cream or throw any socks at me.' He laughs and it feels like all of the horrible stuff that happened has melted away.

'Deal,' we both say simultaneously.

Chapter 23

One year later

'It's moving day,' Sara sings at the top of her voice. I know she's going to miss me really but I also know I've royally outstayed my welcome. 'Who'd have thought it? I can't believe you've been here over a year.' She grins at me as she furiously stuffs the last of my belongings into boxes. Okay I can take a hint.

'I know. I'm so grateful to you for letting me stay for so long.' I go over and give her a big squeeze.

Moving in with Sara was one of the best things that happened to me. It helped me to focus on what I wanted and meant I grew up instead of staying in the safety of my parents' home. I'm so elated to be moving into my own little flat. Somewhere I can put my own stamp on.

I heave my suitcases, which are brimming with clothes that are Sara, Jenna and Denise approved, towards the door. My clothes are no longer drab. When I go out in the evenings now I have plenty of choices and I look pretty good, even if I do say so myself.

I hear a knock at the door and I pull it open eagerly.

It's Jenna, ready and waiting to help me move. The girls are already planning to come over this evening. We're going to order in pizza and have a proper girls' night. I can't wait, it feels so surreal.

'Have you got much more?' Jenna asks eyeing my suitcases and boxes. 'It may take a few trips.' She rolls her eyes and I think back to our trip up to Linkley where she took hardly anything. She likes to travel light, does Jenna.

'No, no this is it.' I had no furniture with me when I moved in. Sara's spare room was already fully decorated and now I'm ready to go out and choose everything afresh for my own place. I have the sofas coming next week and my parents are dropping off a mattress and some essentials later so we'll be camping out on the carpet this evening. Even the idea of sleeping on a mattress on the floor can't dampen my mood, I'm ecstatic. It's certainly been a long journey getting here but it's been worth it.

It's evening and I'm unloading my crockery into the kitchen cupboards when the buzzer goes. I've spent hours cleaning the flat so at least its clean, even if it is untidy.

'Hello?' I say into the intercom. It feels so weird, this flat is my new home.

'Let us in,' Denise, Jenna and Sara shout in unison. They're so loud I physically step back from the intercom; is there a way to turn this thing down? I buzz them in and when I open my front door, they have flowers, a bottle of Prosecco and a small package.

I smile, the welcoming party has arrived.

'Congratulations,' they all shout. Then they're buzzing around the flat saying how good the size is and helping me to imagine where my furniture could go. I'm on cloud nine. The flat is an utter mess and everything is everywhere but I'm so happy to have a place of my own. My own home. We all crowd into the living room where I've cleared a space and put a load of blankets down and draped fairy lights across the walls to make it cosy. We sit around on the floor looking at each other in wonder. It feels really spacious because there's nothing else in here. I've put some music on but the space still feels empty and sounds echoey. I can't wait to really make this my home.

'When is *he* back?' Denise asks smiling.

'A few days.' Lewis is on an art trip with his students in Paris. Lucky him. I wish I was with him but I'm moving into *our* flat instead. Who'd have thought the guy who left me in the loos would be the guy I'm moving in with. 'It's annoying we had to complete on the flat when he was away but you know what it's like.' I shrug, these things never go to plan, I'm just relieved it's all over and we have our home. 'He's excited to get back and get his stuff moved in.'

'Speaking of that we've got some gifts for you.' Sara hands me the flowers and Prosecco. 'This one is for Lewis,' she says grinning from ear to ear. I study my friends with suspicion; what are they up to?

'Okay. I'll give it to him when he's back, what is it?' I ask, wondering what the girls could have bought him. What a sweet gesture.

'So when do you go back to work?' Jenna interrupts, changing the subject.

'Next week and I'm going down to part-time.'

I'm thrilled, I've built up my photography portfolio

and have bookings all through next year which has meant I can pull back at work now. My aim is to quit altogether but I'm so happy I've gone down to three days.

Work have been surprisingly good about my request to go part-time. Liz made a joke about the place falling apart without me that seemed quite genuine, so I'm pleased they've finally realised my worth. It doesn't seem quite so boring now either.

I've been loving getting back into my photography properly. Doing wedding fayres and family portraits has kept me really busy and with a full-time job it was exhausting, but all of my hard work is finally paying off.

Jenna has been a godsend and has signed up for an evening photography course to hone her skills but she definitely has a natural eye for it, which helps. She is my official assistant and Lewis is our videographer at *Moments2Capture* photography and video.

'I'm so pleased for you,' Denise says, giving me a quick hug.

I'm pretty pleased for myself too. A little over a year ago my life was in a completely different place. A dead-end job, living at home, no boyfriend and I'd lost all of my self-worth but thanks to a weird and wonderful weekend away my life has changed forever. I've found myself again and I can't wait to see what happens with the business and life.

'Thank you, I'm so excited to make this flat into our home and start decorating.' I've already planned how I want all the rooms to look, not that there's that many to decorate but we agreed a two bedroom flat would be a good starter home. Before eventually moving onto our forever home. Eek.

The rest of the evening goes by in a flash while we

chat about what everyone is up to. Jenna and Dave are about to go on a romantic getaway, since they sorted everything out they've become like young lovers again. It's actually pretty vomit making sometimes, but sweet. Jenna doesn't know but Dave, who has organised everything, has booked to go back to where they went on their honeymoon, a kind of second honeymoon. It's such a lovely, romantic gesture. He's even arranged for Mum and Dad to have the kids while they're away.

Sara has Mick moving in with her in a couple of weeks' time, Sara has finally committed to someone so I know he's really special. I've got to know Mick quite well over the last year while I've been living at Sara's and he's so lovely. He brings out a much softer side to Sara that I'd never seen before, he has really tamed the beast.

Denise and Jay are getting married, it had been a long time coming but when he popped the question it was a complete surprise to Denise. He proposed to her on a deserted beach in Cornwall, how romantic and lovely. Jenna, Sara and I are her bridesmaids. To think a mere year ago it would have been unfathomable that Jenna would be one of Denise's bridesmaids.

We've all become so much closer over the last year and I've really rekindled my relationship with Jenna. Especially with working together too. We don't always see eye to eye but we tell each other how it is now. We're stronger than ever. Mum and Dad have been so happy to see how close we are.

'Hello, I'm so happy to see you. Let's get back to our new flat.' Lewis can hardly control his excitement. I've picked him up from the school, the bus ride from France must have been a long one and he certainly looks a bit worse for wear, he has a five o'clock shadow and his clothes are crumpled and creased. I haven't had a sniff but I get the distinct feeling he won't be smelling very nice either.

'I bet you can't wait to get back and have a shower,' I say, hinting at where I think his first stop should be.

When we get back to the flat, he has another look around familiarising himself with the layout again and looking at the rooms I've already started painting. He surveys the bedroom with the mattress on the floor and I think about how amazing it is that we'll be picking out all of our bedroom furniture together soon. Lewis has been living in a fully furnished house-share so, like me, he has no furniture to bring, just bags of clothes and other bits and bobs. Sara will be pleased to have us out from under her feet as we spent most of our time at hers rather than at his overcrowded house.

'Lovely flowers,' he says as he passes through the living room and it reminds me of the package the girls left for him.

I hand it over to Lewis and he looks at me puzzled. 'It's from the girls and I have no idea what it is.'

He slowly unwraps it and as he does, I can see his shoulders shake with laughter and he holds his nose. The girls, ever the clowns, have wrapped up the twin to my nephew's sock, the one that we threw at him in the services and it absolutely stinks.

There's a small note which says:

Welcome to the family! We can go for ice cream to celebrate. Here's a sock to go with it.

He looks at me and smiles. I laugh and I love that he has a good sense of humour and can laugh at himself.

Oh, that smile. I could get lost in it. It's so good to have him back even though he's only been gone five days.

It seems like we've known each other for ever and not just for the last year. After our fated meeting in the coffee shop we went on some wonderful dates. We share a love of art and photography that has really brought us together. He has helped challege me, and I him, in everything that we do and I'm so glad that we moved on from indifference and hate, to love.

THE END

About the author

While travelling extensively throughout her twenties Amelia Watchman always had a romcom to hand. After seeing interesting characters and scenarios in her own life she has put pen to paper (well, fingers to keyboard) to write her debut novel Love, Hate and Indifference. She's now busily working on her second novel while also juggling the hungry demands of a toddler and a baby.

Printed by Amazon Italia Logistica S.r.l.
Torrazza Piemonte (TO), Italy

12971458R00112